SPECIAL MESSAGE TO READERS

This book is published under the auspices of

THE ULVERSCROFT FOUNDATION

(registered charity No. 264873 UK)

Established in 1972 to provide funds for research, diagnosis and treatment of eye diseases. Examples of contributions made are: —

A Children's Assessment Unit at Moorfield's Hospital, London.

•

Twin operating theatres at the Western Ophthalmic Hospital, London.

•

A Chair of Ophthalmology at the Royal Australian College of Ophthalmologists.

•

The Ulverscroft Children's Eye Unit at the Great Ormond Street Hospital For Sick Children, London.

You can help further the work of the Foundation by making a donation or leaving a legacy. Every contribution, no matter how small, is received with gratitude. Please write for details to:

THE ULVERSCROFT FOUNDATION,
The Green, Bradgate Road, Anstey,
Leicester LE7 7FU, England.
Telephone: (0116) 236 4325

In Australia write to:

THE ULVERSCROFT FOUNDATION,
c/o The Royal Australian and New Zealand
College of Ophthalmologists,
94-98 Chalmers Street, Surry Hills,
N.S.W. 2010, Australia

RUN WITH THE FOX

In a world of rigid discipline and backbreaking toil, life is tough for Lew Ames at the prison farm. Fellow convict Mel Savage's objective is the recovery of a quarter million dollars. Ames' release date is near — and if he helps Savage, there's a half share of the cash in it for him . . . But when a man runs with the fox he can never expect his life to be easy. For sudden death will follow should his mission fail . . .

Books by Craig Cooper
in the Linford Mystery Library:

BLACKMAIL IS MURDER

CRAIG COOPER

RUN WITH THE FOX

Complete and Unabridged

LINFORD
Leicester

First published in Great Britain by
Robert Hale Limited
London

First Linford Edition
published 2007
by arrangement with
Robert Hale Limited
London

British Library CIP Data

Cooper, Craig
Run with the fox.—Large print ed.—
Linford mystery library
1. Ex-convicts—Fiction 2. Suspense fiction
3. Large type books
I. Title
823.9′14 [F]

ISBN 978–1–84617–789–7

1

Lew Ames straightened his aching back and released his grip on the pick handle for long enough to wipe sweat from his streaming brow with a calloused hand and glance around him at the arid scene. Even after six months of this treatment his body refused to inure itself to the back-breaking toil.

A guard spotted him and spat brittle words at him.

'All right, Ames, you ain't here for a rest cure. Get weaving with that pick, goddamit.'

'Goddamn yourself, Lashley,' Ames gritted under his breath.

'What's that you said, boy?' the thick-chested guard growled and swaggered over.

'I didn't say anything.'

'Goddamn me if you didn't! And you didn't say anything, what?' the man added with a sadistic sneer.

'Sir,' Ames replied from cracked lips.

'Raise your voice so I can hear you, boy.'

'Sir,' Ames cried and glared at the man.

'Get on with it then, you baby-eyed jerk. You got a pick in your hands, boy. You use it for picking with. Get it?'

'Yes, sir.'

'Start picking, baby-eyes, if you don't want to find yourself in the hospital block.'

Ames lowered his head and arched his torso to the task. There had been a momentary suspension of labour on the part of the other men in the immediate vicinity while they took in the exchange. But now they looked at the hot, dry earth and went on with their work.

'Lousy mongrel,' Mel Savage snorted at Ames' back. 'I'd love to rip the mean guts out of him and feed them to the buzzards, if only to see the buzzards drop dead from poisoning.'

'Take it easy, Mel.'

'He keeps riding us, Lew,' Savage grumbled ferociously. 'He'll ride me till I smash the bastard's skull in.'

They were clearing a field that seemed to have a solid rock base. It was divided up into sections, and as soon as one section was cleared to the satisfaction of the overseer, the trucks came from another part of the country that was being exploited for a housing development. These trucks were laden with good rich top-soil and they were emptied into the gaping holes left by the excavation of the rocks.

When the soil was deposited the elderly prisoners in the work team were herded to it with shovels and hoes and rakes, to bed the soil in and break it up fine enough for the planting of seeds.

Once a week gelignite was set to blow away the rock that no amount of picking would remove; afterwards the men with the picks went in, toiling an eight-hour shift in the blazing sunshine. They took a spell at pick-wielding, then changed over with the prisoners loading the buggies which carried the rock to a common pile, there to be lifted by the trucks bringing up the soil and carted back to make foundations for the roads that would serve the housing estates.

Here and there, at strategic intervals,

armed guards watched with thinly-veiled boredom. They had been watching for so long the exercise meant little to them anymore. In any case it was their function to guard the prisoners while the overseer — an agricultural expert — took complete charge of the actual project.

Far down the hill was the compound, the fenced sprawl of huts where the men lived and ate and quarrelled, and longed for the freedom beyond the confines of the prison farm.

There were dogs there too, dogs that would as soon sink their fangs into an escaping convict as into the hunks of meat which were thrown to them once a day.

In the last three months two of the inmates had made their break. They had managed to scale the fence and reach the country road at the border of the woods before Jules Colport, the head warden, had ordered the dogs to be turned loose.

It was the popular belief of the prisoners that Colport had known of the escape bid long before the two men reached the lower wheat field, and had held his hand to let the men imagine they were going to find their freedom. Then the siren whined and the dogs barked, and hut-mates of the luckless escapers looked at each other silently in the darkness and trembled.

Anse Nevin was brought back with the lower half of his body lacerated so badly he had died three days later from the shock. Curt Olsen was carted back dead on one of the guards' horses. Olsen had been shot twice in the chest and then mauled by the dogs.

In the morning Colport made a speech that was both an explanation and a warning. He finished off by relating that during his twenty years at the farm no less than fifteen prisoners had endeavoured to escape.

'Only one made it,' he said with a broad smirk. 'I'll leave it to your imagination what became of the others.'

'The cold-blooded killer,' Savage had murmured to Ames. 'He means to put the fear of death in us.'

'I can feel somebody walking on my

grave at this minute,' Ames had rejoined.

'All the same, Lew, I'm going to get out of here. If I don't I'll go crazy. I believe I am half crazy anyhow. You know how long I've been here, Lew?'

Ames did know. Savage had told him shortly after his arrival at the prison farm. As soon as Savage learned that Ames was in his final year he had begun to cultivate the younger man.

At forty, Savage was a brawny six-footer. He had been in the pen for three years and had been drafted to the prison farm on the strength of his good conduct record. He had been there a year when Ames arrived.

'I've laid my plans well, Lew,' he'd told Ames at the beginning. 'They're going to keep me here for another seven years. They just think! I set my sights on a prison farm and now I've made it. The next step is over the fence and away to the bright blue yonder.'

'Escape?' Ames had queried.

'Why not? Can you tell me some other way? Oh, it's okay for you, pal. You drew a measly two-year stretch for running down somebody when you were drunk. Anybody can get tanked up and kill a pedestrian. You don't have to spend nights dreaming about that fence. But it's all I think of.'

'You'd need help,' Ames had said. 'Where are you going to find it?'

'Friends,' Savage confided. 'Four of them. Take a hard look at me and see if you remember.'

'I don't have to look or strain my memory, Mel. The papers were full of the bank robbery. I recognized you as soon as I hit the place. It was claimed you and your outfit got away with a quarter of a million dollars. You were the only one to get caught. It was tough luck.'

'Tough,' Savage repeated in fierce concentration. 'I was racing for the getaway heap when I collected a slug in the leg. I thought they had killed me. Well, when you catch a big bullet and you're knocked over, you think the very worst. They were going to wait for me but I waved them on. If they'd held back another minute we would all have been caught. As it is, they're free, and the money is safely hidden until I get out of here.'

'You're certainly an optimist, Mel.'

'Look, kid, don't give me that,' Savage snarled. 'I know. I got messages smuggled in when I was in the pen. Eve — that's my girlfriend — knew what she was doing all right. She weighed up the situation right there in the getaway car. Our three pals might just beat it with the dough and leave me to rot, she figured. Oh, Eve is a smart dame, Lew. You know what she did?'

Ames couldn't attempt to guess. Savage, suffused with a warm glow at the memory, had continued to explain.

'The heap got stalled at traffic lights in the centre of Maytown. So Eve, having worked out all the angles, opened the door where she was sitting, grabbed the suitcases containing the dough, and sprang out.'

'She sure took a long chance.'

'She took a gamble, of course. And the very first thing anybody would do would be to jump out after her and go for the cases. But these guys I teamed with didn't lose their marbles. They played it cool, knowing that any kind of excitement would attract the cops and make nonsense of the entire deal.'

'The girl got clear?'

'It worked like a charm for her. She flagged down a cab going in the opposite direction and took off with the suitcases. She told the hack driver to take her to some small cheap hotel and left him to pick one.'

'That was neat thinking.'

'You don't know my Eve, Lew. She can think and then some. She was missing for two days after that while the boys had to lie low at the hideout in case they'd be recognized. When she did turn up at the hideout they wanted to skin her, naturally.'

'But if they did, they would never see their share of that quarter million peanuts.'

'You're a smart guy yourself, Lew. I reckon they tried bouncing Eve to make her talk. But she can be as hard as nails when the necessity arises. She gave them her ultimatum. The dough was hidden and it would remain hidden until they all managed to spring me out of the pen.'

'That's a long time ago, Mel. You know what dames are. They remain faithful for only as long as their glands leave them in peace. I don't want to pour water on your dreams, but you should have a good look at the facts.'

At this Savage had gone for Ames and it had taken two guards to club him off. Savage hadn't looked at him for a week, but finally the breach was healed, as Savage realized it must be healed if he was to use the younger man in the manner he had planned.

'I'm sorry, Lew. I didn't mean to jump at you the way I did. I shot a bolt maybe.'

'You blew your cool, man,' Ames grinned crookedly. 'I'd rather have you for a friend than for an enemy.'

'Do we make it up?'

'If you forgive me what I said about your dame.'

'Sure, I forgive you, Lew. You've never met Eve. So you can't begin to understand the sort of girl she is.'

'She must be some dame, Mel. I've

never met a woman who wouldn't cheat with my best friend. But you're expecting her to wait for ever.'

'Don't let's start that over again,' Savage growled. 'I know what I'm doing. Eve knows what I'll be doing. Planning. She'll be waiting patiently for a sign from me.'

'And sitting on the quarter million?'

'Sitting tight, mister. Make no mistake about it. Look, Lew, are you married?'

'No, sir. Every time I think of marriage, do you know what I see?' Savage was in no way interested in what he saw, but Ames went on to explain all the same. 'I see a door and a key. And do you know who carries the key locked away in her bosom like the last shreds of her virginity?'

'Your private girlfriend?' Savage asked indifferently.

'No special girl, Mel. This dame is a symbol of womankind. The door symbolizes marriage, and the key — '

'You pull yourself together, for pete's sake, Lew. You're going nuts.'

'I'm not,' Ames argued. 'I'm simply

putting forward my views on women and marriage.'

Savage had been extremely patient with him. Ames still had six months to serve and he could afford to be patient. They took up the conversation on another night when the hut was fetid and it was difficult getting to sleep with the groans and wrestlings of the prisoners trapped in nightmares that had no end for them.

'What kind of job did you do, Lew? Some cushy number, I bet. You're a guy with education. You speak well.'

'Thanks for the compliment,' Ames simpered. He shrugged and grinned in the darkness. 'But you're in for a surprise. I was a salesman. A door-to-door boy with a flashing smile and a sweet way with those cheating ladies.'

'Say,' Savage grunted and licked his lips. 'You must have had some rare times. What kind of lays did you get?'

'Please, Mel. I'm young and healthy. The only way I can stay sane is pretend there is only one species on earth.'

'Sure,' the other sympathized. 'But all I think of is Eve. I know she's waiting for me. It's a sort of anchor, you might say.'

'A guy has got to envy you, Mel. I hope you do make your break. I hope that Eve does remain true to you, and that you get your fair share of the quarter million and live happily ever after.'

'Over the rainbow,' Savage murmured reflectively. 'I loved that picture. I loved that little girl with the wonderful voice.'

'She grew up.'

'Yeah,' the big man said sadly. 'There's the hell of it. We're all a parcel of goddamn dreamers, Lew. You don't have much loot stashed by?'

'Not a green dollar bill. Still, I'm young, like I always keep reminding myself, and I'm strong. I've got a little push left.'

A few nights later Savage picked up the threads of the conversation.

'We could do each other a favour, Lew.'

'How come? And you're not going queer in the hot sunshine, mister?'

'Jack it up, mister. I'm talking about afterwards. When you get out of here.'

'I see,' Ames murmured and waited.

'I've got it all figured,' Savage continued with enthusiasm. 'I can get over that fence without a lot of trouble. I've got plenty of wind and my legs are as strong as tree-trunks. I'll run and run till I get to the edge of the woods, where the road is.'

'Don't leave Colport out of your imaginings, friend. Don't forget the dogs either. And hark back to those poor saps who thought they had it made before they were ripped to pieces.'

Savage's craggy face glistened with sweat in the darkness.

'I've thought of it. Every angle. I know I can do it. I know I can make it to the road.'

'So what happens there? A cab comes along with his flag up? Or maybe a bus would give you the really comfortable ride you're considering?'

'A car, Lew,' Savage said slowly while his black eyes glittered on the younger man's.

Here Ames emitted a low whistle.

'You're asking me to have a car there? And find myself back in solitary in a week?'

'You're scared?'

'Damn right I'm scared, Mel. I've had enough of this stuff to do me for a lifetime.'

'You jumped the gun on me just then,' Savage muttered in a disappointed tone. 'It wasn't exactly the way I was planning it.'

'What way were you planning it?'

'First of all you'd find where Eve is at. It wouldn't be such a big job if you went about it the right way.'

'I don't know, Mel.'

'Curse it, Lew, you might be scared. But you aren't completely yellow. You take too many risks with those guards to be yellow. You're full of gutsy spunk.'

At that moment a guard had put his head through the door they hadn't heard open.

'What are you guys talking about?'

Immediately the two men lay down on their bunks and feigned sleep.

Savage grew more eager to get through to Ames. Ames had dropped on to his bunk in the darkness and fallen into a drugged sleep at once. That day Lashley had taken a delight in seeing how far he could be goaded before breaking. Ames had simply increased the tempo of the killing rhythm with his pick. When the stint was over he walked back down the hill like a man in a trance. Every fibre of his physical being throbbed and vibrated, and he was practically asleep before he reached the bunk.

Mel Savage nudged his shoulder from above. He nudged and kept on nudging until Ames stirred.

'Listen, Lew.'

'Leave me alone, Mel.'

'I've just had it, pal. It came to me like a rocket.'

'You know where to stuff it, chum.'

'You don't want to earn yourself a hundred thousand bucks?'

Grimly, Ames shook the torpor from his bloodstream and peered into the face hanging over him.

'Now you figure you're Santa Claus — '

'It's what you'll get, Lew. I promise you. My solemn promise. I had it all worked out to the point where you and Eve have a car on the country road above the fields. But I got stuck there. You see, I couldn't plan how you'd let me know you were there.'

'How?' Ames wondered sleepily.

'Wake up, damn you.'

'I am awake. I said how. But before you tell me how, tell me how I'm going to get in touch with Eve. You haven't got a clue as to where she might be.'

'Oh, yes I have. You'll make for the old hideout. You'll stay there. It's the one solid link still existing between me and Eve. She'll keep making checks. I know how her mind operates. She'll drop by one day and you'll be there. You'll introduce yourself — '

'A letter of introduction?' Ames sneered.

'I'll do it. I'll write a note. One of the guys has got a pencil. That crazy Binson that was an artist. He keeps drawing on the walls, on the floors. I'll get a scrap of paper, or a piece of cloth, even.'

'Don't get steamed up so. Okay, I've got your note and I go to your hideout. I wait. For how long — one year? Five?'

Savage gnashed his teeth in frustration.

'A month will do it. Maybe a week. But

you'll stay there anyhow. It will be worth it in the end, Lew. Just think of it, mister. A hundred grand!'

'My head's swimming. I've got your note, like I said. So Eve happens along. What do we do next?'

'You pick on a day. The sooner the better. You'll drive out on the road and you'll blow on the car horn. You can hear a pin drop around noon. Make it noon.'

'What will that mean?'

'It'll mean I'll be making for the road at midnight on the following day. It's a cinch, Lew. We can't lose.'

'If Colport doesn't shoot you in the back. If the dogs don't rip your throat out.'

'Will you do it, Lew?'

'Okay,' Ames said after a while. 'But I'll do worse afterwards if I don't collect that hundred grand.'

2

A violent rocking brought Ames awake. He opened his eyes stupidly in the gloom and saw a heavy-jowled man bending over him. The man was one of the guards and his name was Arliss.

'It isn't daylight yet.'

'Nobody mentioned daylight,' Arliss said in a thick whisper. 'You get to your feet. Make any fuss and you'll wish it's graves you're digging out there.'

His brain a welter of confusion, Ames struggled from his bunk and drew on his trousers.

'Never mind your shoes.'

Ames didn't like the sound of that, but there was absolutely nothing he could do. If he yelled or made a fuss he would only suffer the more for it.

Arliss shoved him over the earthen floor to the door. On his bunk Mel Savage lay and watched with bated breath.

'You poor bastard, Lew,' he murmured when the door closed on the guard and his friend. 'You don't know what they're taking you out there for.'

Ames soon knew. In the shadows of the compound he saw another guard, and then yet a third one came round the corner of the hut.

'Bring him over here,' Burt Lashley said softly.

'No!' Ames panted. 'You can't. Take me to the head warden. You can't get away with it.'

He struggled when the two men gripped him and thrust him across the baked earth of the compound. He was as big as either of them and as strong, but against the both of them he knew he would stand no chance.

They dragged him to the outhouse where the field equipment was stored and each of the men took hold of a wrist until he was spreadeagled against the wall. The moon was drifting in an ocean of pale fluffy clouds. One of the dogs barked furiously on the perimeter of the compound. For Ames it was a horrible nightmare scene.

Lashley flung his hat to the ground and rolled up his sleeves. The man on Ames' right made some sort of gurgling sound in his throat.

Lashley waded in. He had been building up to this all day and now he allowed his bitterness and his anger, and all the other frustrated emotions he was capable of, spill out in a frenzy of action.

He battered Ames with his fists until he couldn't stand. When he crumpled at the knees the two guards hauled him upright and the panting Lashley renewed his punishment. Ames never knew when the sadist desisted.

Later he was gathered up like a sack of flour and hauled back to his bunk.

In the morning Ames was a sorry sight.

They prodded him to tell him it was daylight and he had a date in the fields in fifteen minutes.

'What are you trying to do to him?' Mel Savage roared. 'Kill him?'

'Clam up, mister. If you guys want to spend the night fighting amongst yourselves, what can you expect but one of you to get hurt?'

A seething retort leaped to Savage's lips, but he bit it down in time. He would share some of the medicine handed out to Ames, and that wouldn't help either of them.

'He can't go into the fields,' he maintained stubbornly. 'Can't you see that his jaw is broken?'

The guard stared down at the unconscious Ames and looked worried. 'We'll get him to the hospital bay. Okay, you fish-eyed sons of bitches, mind your own business and clear out of here.'

Ames came to in a small room with white walls and a low ceiling. He was sure there wasn't a bone or muscle in his body that Lashley hadn't accounted for. He tried to raise his head in order to look around him, and it seemed a dozen convicts were addressing themselves to his skull with hammers.

He was lying on some sort of bed; only it wasn't really a bed either, but what he took to be a crude operating table. When he attempted to shout a protest, pain flamed into his lower left jaw, and the sound he emitted was a garbled croak. He needn't bother to shout anyhow, as there was no one else in the room to listen to him.

The door of the room opened and Jules Colport came to stand at his side and stare at him. Colport was wearing a neatly-pressed grey uniform. He had shaved and given himself a manicure, and he buffed off his nails on the cuffs of his jacket as he stared impersonally for a half minute.

He had tiny blue eyes trapped in deep sockets, and a mouth that was both sensual and cruel. A sneer warped the thick lips.

'What happened to you?'

'I was beaten.' Talking was a great effort for Ames, but he managed it by trying not to move his jaws.

'Who beat you?'

'It happened in the darkness.'

'In your quarters?'

Ames nodded his agreement.

'There was a fight. You didn't see who it was who attacked you?'

Ames moved his head from one side to the other.

'Then you couldn't identify your attackers?'

'No, I couldn't.'

Satisfaction glowered in the small eyes.

'The doctor is going to look at you.'

Colport went out and a tall, slim man in a white coat came into the room. He closed the door behind him, then went to work on Ames. He handled him with a gentleness that was totally alien to the environment, and those who inhabited it.

'The jaw isn't broken,' he said after a time. 'In fact you're very lucky in that you've no broken bones at all. Am I registering clearly with you?'

Puzzled, Ames found the concerned eyes and inclined his head.

'It was the guards, wasn't it?'

Ames didn't reply to this. It could be a trick, he realized, cooked up by the medico and Colport.

'You don't have to be scared, Lew. My name is Fletcher. I know who you are. Colport doesn't know, naturally. I could easily tell him if you've had enough. It's tough going at this joint. I never knew how tough it could be.'

Still Ames held his tongue. Fletcher brought a wallet from his pocket and held it open under Ames' nose. Ames let loose with a shuddering sigh.

'Don't try to use your jaws yet, Lew,' Fletcher advised him. 'Your jaw isn't broken, but I'm saying it is. You'll be confined to sick bay for a week at least. You'll be brought in here every morning for an examination. I'm going to prepare a report that will fool Colport. How's it going anyhow?'

Six months had conditioned Ames to the point where he almost did believe he was a convict. In the next few seconds he tried all he knew to orient himself. Fletcher appeared to understand. He smiled and laid a hand on his shoulder.

'Then they wonder what can happen to our guys behind the Iron Curtain. Okay. I'm not rushing you. We'll take it gradually. But you still have a grip on yourself?'

'Sure,' Ames' grin was meagre. 'But I'd rather get back to the hut. At this stage we can't afford to take risks.'

'There's no risk. Your friends saw

clearly the condition you were in. Some of them have shared the same treatment, and they can figure out the shape you're in. Look, no more talking for the present. You're going to rest up, bozo.'

'Colport might suspect something.'

'Colport can go kick his fanny, Lew. I'm in charge of sick bay for three months and Colport's going to have to toe the line with me.'

'You're an angel in disguise, pal.'

'Oh, I don't know. The disguise bit, I mean. All my best buddies figure I'm naturally angelic.'

Ames was lodged in the hospital block, and each morning two orderlies wheeled him through to the consulting room where Wilf Fletcher actually did give him an overhaul.

'We've got to keep your strength running,' the medico gagged. 'You've a long, hard trail in front of you.'

'You'll spoil it if you don't send me back to the hut.'

'Soon,' the other rejoined. 'As I told you, Lew, I'm your boss for the time being.'

'I can talk pretty good at the moment.'

'There's plenty of swelling there yet. I'll let you talk in the morning.'

On the following morning Colport followed Fletcher into the consulting room. Colport had an ugly air about him that Ames noticed at once.

'I'd be the last one to advise you on how to carry out your job, Doctor,' was his bleak preamble. 'But it seems to me that the prisoner is in reasonable shape.'

'You might think so, Warden, but I don't. He nearly died. His heart was beginning to falter somewhat.'

'If that's so, I guess he ought to go back where he came from. This is no place for an unfit man.'

Ames was certain that Fletcher had torn the bottom out of his assignment, and the last thing he wanted was the necessity to divulge his real identity and the nature of his task at the prison farm. Colport wasn't the type who would sit back and be ridden over by officialdom. He would demand an explanation as to why he wasn't consulted at the outset. He would fear too that his methods of handling the camp were liable to be passed up the scale, so that drastic repercussions could follow. This wasn't the ideal atmosphere sought by Ames. Rumours would break out and filter through to the prisoners themselves, when his plan might be greatly endangered.

'I didn't mean he isn't fit. But whatever shock he received annoyed his ticker.'

'They fight like animals. I thought it was his jaw you were concerned with.'

'Warden, am I to take it that you don't agree with how I perform my duties?'

'I didn't say that.'

'Good. Then please leave me to it.'

Colport went out and slammed the door behind him. Fletcher winced momentarily, but his face began flushing with anger.

'Did he mention animals?'

'It's like a zoo, Wilf. I'm not kidding you. Some of these places ought to be cleaned out with a shovel. The guards have forgotten what it's like being human.'

'Can we really blame them?' Fletcher

wondered. 'They aren't handling kindergarten fodder. You become case-hardened to anything. Look at yourself. I bet you're beginning to think like a criminal.'

'I've taught myself to think like a criminal,' Ames responded. 'It's the only way to work this deal.'

'The old tongue is warbling plenty this morning,' Fletcher chuckled. 'How do you feel, partner?'

'Like a nice drink of lime juice,' Ames grinned. 'With lots of ice.'

'My, but we do have a reformed character on our hands. Maybe we should tell Colport so he'll see the value of his tactics. Seriously, Lew, I'd like a report. How are you making out with Savage?'

'Sweet,' Ames said. 'It took him a while to make up his mind about trusting me. At this present minute he'd trust me with his life.'

'How about the dough? Did he give you any indication what happened to it?'

Ames told Fletcher the whole story. When he was through Fletcher remained thoughtful for a long time.

'Then it depends on this dame,' he said

finally. 'It isn't much to latch on to, is it? I mean, they've been apart for a few years. A dame is a dame. She might have grown tired of waiting and decided to make hay with some other guy. Bang goes that quarter million bucks.'

'Savage is certain she'll remain true to him. I believe him when he says the girl took off with the money and hid it. It's reasonable too to suppose that the three guys in the outfit will have applied plenty of pressure to get her to talk. Only Savage says she's capable. She digs her heels in and they stay dug. There is another angle also that plays into our hands,' Ames continued. 'If Eve did get the notion to take off with somebody else, she'd have the three guys to reckon with. That would make her doubly careful. It would cramp her style effectively.'

'She might take off with one of the three,' Fletcher said. 'They could dream up some sort of plot.'

'You're bent on spoiling it for me, Wilf.'

'I hope it isn't spoiled. But your way seems clear enough. Get this note from Savage at the earliest opportunity. See he provides it during my term here at the camp. As soon as you have it, the chief will pull strings to free you.'

Ames shook his head firmly.

'No, Wilf.'

'What do you mean, no? You aren't a masochist by some chance? It'll save time. It'll let you get weaving with the rest of the plan. You can go to the hideout and wait. If Savage is right about the dame, she'll turn up inside of a month. If he's wrong, it'll let us know that much earlier, when we can concentrate on a different angle. As it is, you're going to go on putting up with things at this joint. You don't have to, Lew.'

'I'm playing it my way,' Ames said stubbornly. 'I've got a free hand to do so, and I'm doing it.'

'You'll be back in that hut in the morning. Have you figured it out? More back-breaking labour. Weeks of it. Months of it. Have Savage hustle it up and we'll have you sprung.'

Ames shook his head doggedly. Fletcher whistled softly and scratched his cheek.

'You're the most conscientious agent I

ever did see,' he announced in perplexity.

'I set my sights on this, Wilf. I'm going to pull it off if it's possible. Savage isn't to be underestimated. If he gets really desperate, or if he imagines I'm pulling a bluff on him, he might take it into his head to make the break under his own steam.'

'How far would he get?'

'That's beside the point. It could foul it up at the girl's end. I've got the gag running sweetly and it isn't going to be soured up for any reason.'

'Last word?'

'The very last. Thanks, Wilf. It was great to see you. But make sure that no strings are pulled. Impress on the chief that I know what I'm doing.'

A brief smile brightened Fletcher's solemn features. He held out his hand.

'Put it there, hero. Back to the saltmines.'

* * *

The next day Ames was back with the prisoners. He might have had an infectious disease for the way they shied clear of him.

'What's with these puritans?' he murmured to Savage who had gravitated to him like he was his sole hope of salvation.

'Aw, let the cows' tits huff,' Savage said derisively. 'You can hardly blame them in a way. Lashley has his knife stuck deep in you, Lew, and they don't want to be lined up as your sympathisers.'

Ames looked into the rugged face of the big man. He wondered what grade Savage would have made had he started off on a different path. It reminded him of a story by O. Henry, where a man was led along different roads of destiny. What shaped a man's destiny anyhow? How much say did he have in the shaping of it? A good home background was a help. A good education was a help also. Given these, was there any cause for a man to turn anti-social? It was too great a problem for Ames to solve to his satisfaction.

'What about you, Mel? You aren't exactly in Lashley's book of pin-ups.'

'I'm not a yellow-belly either,' Savage snorted. 'And give me one chance at Lashley. Just give me one chance!'

'What would you do, Mel?'

'I'd pick his heart out,' was the gruff response. 'He's only a gutless beast. But you want a word of advice, friend?' he added on a more sober note.

'Stay out of Lashley's hair? Don't tell me.'

For a week the guard could see nobody else but Ames. He harried him from dawn till dusk. Ames girded himself and pretended it didn't matter. There was too much at stake to allow himself to be drawn into a showdown with Lashley. He could have it called off anytime, he knew. But he had gone too far and taken too much to be thrown off his course by the man.

Savage clung to him closer than ever. In an odd fashion the beating-up taken by Ames had increased his stature in the criminal's eyes. It was as though he had no doubts left concerning Ames' ability and willingness to do what he wanted him to do after his discharge. Also, Savage saw in Ames his one ray of hope, and he never ceased to impress on the younger man how he would benefit by the hundred thousand dollars he had promised him.

'You'll really do it, Lew? I mean, you won't allow anything to sidetrack you once you get out of here?'

'You have my word for it. A hundred grand would give me the right lift in life I need.'

One night Savage slipped Ames the note he had prepared.

'Put it in a safe place,' he enjoined. 'It's your ticket to a hunk of the loot.'

'I hope it goes okay, Mel.'

'I tell you it will go okay. I feel it in my bones. I get hunches, pal, and seldom do they miss.'

'There's just one final point,' Ames said.

'Tell me.'

'I go to the hidout and I wait. I wait for a month and nothing happens. I might wait for two months and nothing happens.'

Mel Savage's eyes glittered brightly in the darkness.

'We can still have a deal,' he said gently. 'You get a heap and come blow your horn. The next night we take off. Then we hunt for the money together. Then the split will be fifty-fifty. Straight down the middle. Think about it, Lew. Think well.'

'Sure,' Ames muttered. 'I'll think about it.'

3

Ames rose early that morning. He showered and shaved, taking twice as long over his ablutions as he would normally have done. It was wonderful luxuriating in soap and water, and the bed he had passed the night in had been a leaf out of Paradise Regained.

When he had dressed he stood at the window of his bachelor apartment and looked down at the busy street below him. It had taken a year at the prison farm to give him a real appreciation of the pleasures of freedom. But he had survived it and that was that. The first stage in the manoeuvre had been successfully completed, and if the rest went as well he might see the assignment to a successful conclusion.

'Eve,' Savage had written in his awkward scrawl, 'this fellow is called Lew Ames, and he's a buddy of mine. He'll tell you all about it. Listen good to what he says and do what he tells you to do. I trust him and so should you.' The note was signed, 'Mel'.

Placing a cigarette between his lips, Ames had a final look at his reflection in a mirror before leaving the apartment and riding the six floors to the street in the elevator.

There was a diner not far away where he ordered a large breakfast and ate it down to the last crumb. With another cigarette in his lips he headed outside and stood on the crowded street to stare around him.

He was thinking in terms of a cab when he noticed the blue Buick at the kerb and recognized it immediately. The Buick was washed and polished until it shone like a rare diamond. He was strolling to the car as a thin man in a grey suit left a doorway and came over to him.

'Guess who?' he said at Ames' back.

'Well, for pete's sake! If it isn't Bunny. I've got you to thank for nursing my buggy?'

'You can thank me for bringing it here. Hop in and I'll drive you to headquarters.

Afterwards you can do your own driving.'

'If it's all the same to you, I'll drive, Bunny,' Ames smiled. 'I haven't practised in a long time.'

'It's why I was going to do the honours,' Bunny grinned. 'I don't want to get plastered over a wall so early in the day. It's bound to take the edge off it.'

It was good to settle behind the wheel of a car again, just as it was good to be able to straighten your shoulders and look around you without having Burt Lashley barking in your ears. The prison farm seemed little better than a remote memory, which proved he was as resilient and adaptable as he'd ever been.

'What are you laughing at?' Bunny said at his side. 'You're only half-way to headquarters. We could still finish up being gathered on a shovel.'

'Don't mention shovel, chum. Don't mention pickaxe. Don't mention a dog barking.'

'You really had a ball. Was it worth it, Lew?'

'I don't know,' Ames replied honestly. 'But time holds the key and time will tell.'

They arrived at the old brownstone building in the city's main street and Ames parked the car.

'Now, lookit, Lew, that thing on the sidewalk is what you call a hydrant in our language. You stop here and you'd be surprised how you attract cops. Take it to the parking area round back.'

'I could drive for a year,' Ames said with a chuckle and patted the steering wheel. 'Watch this for a three-point turn.'

'You poor, poor kid.'

Ames parked on the restricted space at the rear of the building. Bunny Lewis left him there with a firm handshake and Ames walked round to the street and climbed the century-old steps to the long corridor which confronted him.

There was a flight of stairs too that he mounted to a narrower corridor, where he came to the door of the chief's office and rapped before entering.

'Good morning, sir. I hope I'm not too late.'

'Good morning, Lew. No, you're not late at all, as a matter of fact. Take a seat, won't you. Cigar?'

‘Thanks,’ Ames said. He accepted one of the thick cigars from the box on the cluttered desk and sank down on a chair opposite the chief.

The desk had a battery of six telephones on it. Besides these was an intercommunication set, an old, heavily-built typewriter, and a pile of the morning newspapers. The office itself was no larger than fifteen by fifteen. The walls were decorated with maps — mostly large-scale breakdowns — like those in the offices of police headquarter transport details. There was an ancient print of the Rocky Mountains that had been hanging there — a note of supreme incongruity — since the first day Ames had met Edward Ogden, and he would have taken a bet on the print being there twenty years before that.

Ogden himself was a short, compactly built man of around forty-five or so. He was going prematurely bald, and as a gesture of protest, perhaps, had begun cultivating thick sideburns and an ’eighties era moustache. He had a rather pale complexion, a long, wide-bridged nose that flared out into wider nostrils, and the small darting eyes of a confidence trickster.

Those eyes darted over Lew Ames now, noting how the dark-haired young man had lost at least twenty pounds since he'd last seen him, noting how the handsome features had acquired a mahogany-like tan that contrasted sharply with his own sallowness. Still, he thought, Ames looked very fit and very healthy. Nevertheless, Ogden ripped a prepared slip of paper from a pad at his elbow and flipped it across the desk. Ames lifted it and glanced at it. An amused smile plucked at his mouth.

'Is this a joke, sir?'

'It's no joke, Lew. You know as well as I do how a pretty looking wall can conceal all manner of weaknesses inside.'

'But I'm not carrying a pretty looking wall around, and I feel great inside.'

'All the same,' Ogden said with finality, 'you're having a check up. Be at the clinic at two o'clock this afternoon.'

'I guess I'll have to humour you, sir.'

'You're not humouring anybody,' the

squat man snapped. His features relented immediately and he thrust his hand out to Ames. 'Welcome home.'

'Thank you, sir.'

'Fletcher gave me a complete run-down concerning the information you passed on to him,' Ogden said. 'Did anything change materially since to alter the overall picture?'

'Everything went as it should have gone. I gained Mel Savage's total confidence. He prepared a note of introduction to the girl. Her name is Evelyn Birchall. Her three friends are Dave Huggins, Milo Farland, and Art Macklin.'

'I'll have them checked against our list. I may be able to give you something on them when you return this afternoon.'

Here Ogden paused for long enough to select a cigar from his box. He searched for a lighter or match, and Ames struck a match for him and held it under the cigar until it was puffed alight. Then Ogden sank back on his chair and regarded the man before him soberly.

'I've got a suggestion to make, Lew. I'd

like you to listen to it.'

Ames frowned slightly.

'Of course. But I've got my moves planned.'

'I was considering pulling you off the assignment at this stage,' Ogden began slowly. 'You've done your bit and then some. You've got an introductory note. You've got a clue as to where you should lay your bait for this woman?'

'I know the exact location of the old hideout. But, sir, you can't — '

'Let me finish, Lew. the way I see it, you could do with a break. I've got a nice cosy assignment lined up. I was going to put Walton in to replace you. Walton would become you. He would carry on from where you leave off. Nobody could contradict him. He is a good man also, Lew, and — '

Ogden stopped speaking when Ames stood up and extended the palms of both hands. The palms were horny and calloused, like those of a man who had spent all of his life wielding a shovel or a pickaxe.

'I dare say Walton could show you

hands like these?'

'Oddly enough, that facet hasn't been overlooked,' Ogden said in a cold voice. 'Walton has been in training. He's as brown as you are. He's managed to have his hands suitably roughened.'

'But there is a subtle difference, sir. I bear the genuine brandmarks. What I have on my body can't be duplicated by phoney means. This is a quarter-million bank haul at stake. These are tough cookies we're dealing with. They won't be dumb. They won't be easily taken in. Supposing they get really curious with Walton and ask him to tell them bedtime stories of life in a prison camp? Walton might have been cramming on lurid books, but I don't have to be anything but my natural self. I think like a criminal. I talk like a criminal. I've got the necessary chip on my shoulder against society. I've lived with Mel Savage. Mel Savage was my buddy for a whole year. I know how many times he turns in his cot nights, the key he snores in, the kind of dreams that tortured him and brought him awake gibbering.'

Ames took a deep breath and continued in a lower voice.

'Shall I go on, sir?'

'Please don't, Lew. But I had to make doubly certain that your enthusiasm isn't on the wane.'

The intercom buzzed and Ogden depressed the switch.

'Yes, Daisy?'

'Number three, Mr Ogden.'

Ogden lifted the receiver and spoke into the mouth-piece. 'Who is it? Oh, you George. How is it coming? Ahuh! Good boy. Ahuh! Yeah, take it easy, George. Give them all the rope they need. Keep in touch, will you?'

Ogden hung up and placed his cigar back between his teeth.

'Where were we, Lew? Oh, yes. Look, go into one of the anterooms and type out a full report, will you? Right up to date. Bring it to me when you're finished. Go to the clinic at two, like I told you. Come straight back here. When are you going to leave town?'

'I'd like to leave day after tomorrow,' Ames said, his features beaming now.

'Any drastic break in the continuity might prove damaging.'

'It's your baby, Lew. If anything slips you know what the emergency number is.'

'Sure,' Ames said. He rose and turned to the door. 'Thank you for letting me have the baby, sir.'

'Okay. So don't forget the doc. A healthy mother, a healthy baby, they say. Don't forget to collect your cheque either.'

The intercom was buzzing once more as Ames left the office.

A half hour later he was leaving the building, having prepared his report and left it with the chief and having collected his fat pay-cheque. He was tempted to go round for the Buick and take it out to the highway for a flat-out drive. But too well he saw the hazards of indulging his whims. The job was not finished by a long chalk. He didn't know Evelyn Birchall to see. He didn't know Huggins or Farland or Macklin. But it didn't necessarily follow that if any of them should see him driving around Delton City in a swank car the memory wouldn't register later. Of course he could laugh it off and argue that it hadn't been him, but it would make for a weak link in the chain that he could do without.

The hideout he was supposed to go to was a hundred and fifty miles from Delton City, but this fact didn't give a guarantee of none of the gang being in Delton City at the moment.

Round at the parking area he found Bunny Lewis leaning over the hood of the Buick.

'Are you going to take her for the spin?'

'No, Bunny. I've changed my mind. I guess she'll have to go into dry dock for another spell.'

'I'll offer you five hundred bucks for it, Lew.'

'You're nuts,' Ames grinned. 'Take good care of it for me. Oh, say, know any reasonable used car dealers in town?'

'Why not? You want a beat-up to go someplace interesting?'

'You've got the idea.'

'Let's go then. Hop in and I'll drive. Anybody can bum a lift.'

'I want to go to the bank first of all.'

'Let's go there too. I kind of like banks. They look so stout and safe. Only when they're robbed.'

'Boy, oh boy,' Ames chuckled. 'How you do get the drift.'

Bunny drove him to his bank where he deposited his pay-cheque and drew out six hundred dollars. From there his comrade took him to a used car lot. After a half-hour's haggling with the dealer he and Ames settled on a five-year old Dodge. It looked decrepit enough, but had a sound engine and good tyres.

'I still say four hundred bucks is too much,' Lewis told the dealer. 'You'll tank her up with gas?'

'Naturally.'

'How about insurance?' Bunny said.

'I take care of everything,' the dealer told him. 'Give me an hour or so and call back. Deal?'

'Yeah,' Ames agreed. 'Thanks, mister.'

'Where to now?' Bunny wanted to know when they drove out of the used car lot. 'Did you keep enough dough for essentials?'

'Just about. I can't go around heeled, can I?'

'You don't want to starve either. Like I said, where to now? I'm doing nothing much today. Let me treat you to a blowout.'

'Thanks, pal. Bring me home and drop me off. Then look after my buggy.'

Lewis dropped him outside his apartment building and shook hands with him.

'Glad to have met you again, Lew. If you can't be good be hellish careful.'

'You bet, hombre. See you.'

At a quarter to two Ames took a cab to the clinic where he handed over the slip given him by Edward Ogden.

'Thank you, Mr Ames,' the receptionist said. 'I think the doctor is expecting you. I won't keep you a moment.'

She was a trim brunette, with a nice sense of poise and a marvellous figure. She must have felt the intensity of Ames' gaze on her back, for she turned before opening a white-painted door and gave him a warm smile. Ames smiled broadly. I've been living like a goddamn monk, he thought. I really did imagine there was only one species left on earth.

'The doctor will see you immediately, Mr Ames.'

'Thanks, honey. You won't go away?'

She blushed but looked pleased, and her warm smile followed him until he vanished beyond the white door.

He was given a rigorous overhaul, from the toes up. Later the medico told him to get dressed and sat down at a small desk to make notes.

'How did I make out, Doc?'

'If there is such a thing as a perfect specimen, Mr Ames, then you're it.'

'He?' Ames chuckled.

'My ideal comes with a finer grain of skin, and with a lot more curves than you've got.'

'Mine too, Doc, if you want to hear the truth.'

The receptionist was waiting in her pink and brown cubicle. She accepted the notes which Ames gave her.

'These will proceed to the proper quarters immediately, Mr Ames.'

'That's what I call efficiency, honey. Don't you ever relax, though?'

'Occasionally. But usually after hours.'

'Say around eight o'clock in the evening?'

'Could be.' Dimples showed in her cheeks. 'But you don't even know my name.'

'You'd look good under any name, honey. But what is it?'

'Doris, Doris Kattner.'

'And you're just bound to have an address,' Ames grinned. 'Well, I've got to know where to pick you up at eight.'

She told him and Ames said so-long and left her. He took a cab back to headquarters and found he would have to wait for thirty minutes before the chief was free. At length he was asked to step into his office.

'Well, you're cleared, Lew,' Edward Ogden informed him. 'Of course it was nothing but a matter of form.'

'Of course, sir. Did you dig up anything on our subjects?'

'Just Farland,' the chief explained and consulted a sheet of paper in front of him. 'He was arrested for attempting a gas-station holdup in 'sixty-eight.'

'A solo effort that was aborted?'

'A solo effort. It happened in Basingville. He drew a six months' sentence. That doesn't sound too good, does it?'

'It sounds like the gang could have broken up,' Ames murmured frowningly. 'Still, Basingville is a mere two-fifty, three hundred miles from here. While there's life there's hope.'

'Give it a whirl anyhow, Lew. My private opinion is that they have broken up. The woman could have gone off someplace with somebody. A man in prison is a poor thing to go to bed with nights.'

'Agreed. But what about the quarter million?'

'Yes,' Ogden said heavily, 'what about the quarter million? Try and find out about it.'

'No limit to time?'

'We decided that at the outset. Every so often somebody in Washington wants to light a fire under my tail. I ask for patience. We work patiently and carefully. The results we get justify the means we employ.'

A short time afterwards Ames was leaving the old building once more. He took another cab to the used-car lot and learned that the Dodge was ready for him.

That night he saw Doris Kattner. She lived up fully to his expectations. She didn't leave him until an hour before she was due to start work at the clinic next morning.

'When do I see you again, Lew?' she wondered.

'I wish it could be soon, baby, but it can't be. Next time I need a checkup, perhaps?'

'I might be in an old folks' home by then.'

'Then where will I be? No, I'm not kidding. At the very earliest date. Goodbye, doll.'

The next day he left Delton City in the beatup Dodge.

4

In the gathering dusk he left a small hamlet called Boynton behind him. He had eaten a solid meal there, tanked up the Dodge once more, and now, by his reckoning, he shouldn't have much further to go.

There was a lake in the open country, Mel Savage had explained. It was called Looking Glass Lake, and when he found it he had only to climb a hill, turn on to a dirt track off the main road, and a mile or so along he would come to the old house.

In Ames' estimation, the main road he was travelling was little better than a dirt track. In Boynton he had mentioned the lake to a local, gesturing to a shotgun in the rear of the car. He said he had heard there was duck-shooting to be had.

'Well, I don't know about ducks,' the yokel had sniggered. 'But there are some of the fattest rats up there you ever did see.'

'Rats or ducks,' Ames rejoined equably. 'I'll get a shot anyhow.'

Out here was poor prairie country, dotted here and yonder in the distance with small sod-buster farms. Off to the west the hills sprawled in a haze of bright crimson and gold. The air felt good at any rate, a trifle chill at this hour of the day, but muggy enough in the hollows where the day's heat remained trapped.

The road before him was a punishing switchback, dipping and climbing and tapering off yellowishly, to infinity, it seemed.

Ames had brought a half-dozen cans of beer along, as well as a five-gallon plastic container of fresh water. One thing he'd never forget about the prison camp was the warm, acrid-tasting water.

He saw the lake after a while and stalled the Dodge to reach in behind him and open one of the beer cans. Looking Glass Lake was a huge oval, ringed by fir trees, and in the waning light it did appear as a giant, dull-surfaced mirror.

Ames drank the beer, lit a cigarette, and batted the brim of his soft hat away from his forehead. He switched on the motor and climbed a long and gradual hill. At the top of it he saw a narrower track snaking off through the bunchgrass on his left. The track was stony and rutted, and he was surprised to see a field of stubbly wheat when he had travelled another mile.

Presently a gaunt timber and brick two-storied house rose out of the shadows on his right. There was a gateway leading to a wide yard, and when he'd stalled at the entrance he saw a light glowing through flimsy window curtains. At that instant a dog commenced a harsh, wicked barking that caused the hairs to bristle at the nape of his neck.

The dog leaped from the narrow front porch and was brought up abruptly with a length of chain. It scrabbled to gain its feet, raised its head and went on barking.

'Shet up, Whitey!'

A man had appeared in the doorway with the soft light from an oil lamp spilling out behind him. He had a rifle, or shotgun, in his hands and the muzzle was pointed at Ames's car.

Ames got out slowly.

'Good evening,' he said.

'Howdy. Have you missed your way?' The voice was shrill and thin.

'I don't think so. I was told back in the village that I'd find a house about here.'

'So you've found it. My name's Dobbs. You looking for me, by any chance?'

'Not exactly.'

'What do you want then?'

'Well . . . ' Ames floundered for a moment, wondering how to cope with the unexpected situation. Here was something that Savage hadn't allowed for, no more than he had.

'You've got to be a stranger.'

'That's right,' Ames said, willing to grasp at any straw. 'I happen to be on vacation. Left the big city behind and came out here to fill my lungs with air, and maybe do a little shooting. I stopped in the village, and a man said I might get put up here.'

There was a moment of thoughtful silence. Then, 'This ain't a hotel.'

'I know it isn't an hotel. I came to get

away from hotels. Say, do you live alone, Mr Dobbs?'

'What's it to you if I do?' was the suspicious response. 'You haven't got any fresh ideas?'

Ames laughed and the dog began barking afresh. Dobbs kicked it in the ribs and it yelped and cringed down on the porch.

'Shet your goddamn mouth,' he scrowled. 'What's so funny, mister?'

'Nothing. My name is Ames. Lew Ames. You've got a sharp watchdog there.'

'Yeah. You figure on any fancy tricks and he'll have a bite out of your ass quicker'n you can think.'

'Then I can't come in? You haven't got a room to spare? I wouldn't expect much. A bunk and a bite of chuck in the mornings.'

'You wouldn't get much,' Dobbs said.

'I could drive back to the village and bring food.'

Another thoughtful silence while Dobbs mulled it over.

'I'm willing to pay,' Ames added.

‘What gave you the idea to pick on my place?’

‘Nothing special. Okay, Dobbs, if you don’t want visitors, you don’t want them.’

Ames turned back to his car.

‘Wait,’ Dobbs said. ‘No need to hurry. I gotta be careful. A lot of bums come past in the summer. One day I had a carload of hippies. They were all high and they tied me up in the bedroom. Ate everything in the house and drank my liquor.’

‘You didn’t have Whitey then?’

‘Hell with Whitey. The hippies gave him something that made him curl up and go to sleep.’

‘You can see I’m not a hippie.’

‘Yeah, I can. You don’t talk like one anyhow. All right, stranger. Come ahead in and I’ll rustle you something.’

‘Whitey won’t bite, like you said?’

‘Naw. He only makes that hellawful noise when somebody drops by, which ain’t often. Guess he didn’t go for the sleeping drops the hippies gave him.’

Ames got into the Dodge and drove it on through the gateway entrance. He parked it in the yard with the nose pointing towards the road. Then he lifted out the remaining cans of beer and locked the car.

'You care for beer, Mr Dobbs?'

'Now and again,' Dobbs said carefully. Up close Ames realized he wasn't quite as old he'd imagined. Fifty to fifty-five, he guessed. He stepped over the dog and went in front of the man into the house.

It was a typical farmhouse, Ames saw, with a large, high-ceilinged kitchen and wide, open fireplace. It was sparsely furnished, but clean. A Navajo rug adorned one wall; on another hung a large print of Lincoln. A huge rush mat covered the centre of the floor. Cooking was done by bottled gas, Ames noted. The stove was littered with cooking utensils. Dobbs continued to regard him silently as Ames laid the beer cans on the table.

'Go ahead and help yourself.'

'Too late for beer-drinking. I never drink much after seven or eight. Never eat much either, come to that. My innards would act up on me if I did.'

Dobbs showed him to a bathroom at

the back and said he would get a meal going if he was hungry.

'I'm not hungry. I had a meal in the village before coming on here.'

'You said you were gonna do shooting. Where's your gun?'

'Out in the car. Don't worry. It's locked.'

Later Dobbs took him upstairs to a bedroom. It was at the front of the house, and by daylight he'd have a good view of the surrounding countryside.

'How long were you figuring on staying?'

'How long could you have me?' Ames asked cautiously.

'Suit yourself,' the man shrugged. 'It gets damn lonesome living out here all on your own. I'm not sure why I bought the house. I used to have a wife, you see. But she upped and died. I never really knew why. I'm a farmer. Always was a farmer. Got chickens shut up out back. If you didn't shut them in at night you wouldn't have many left come morning. They lay eggs. Got four cows and they give milk. Three of them do anyhow. Then I grow a few crops. Few potatoes, beans, stuff like that.'

'Sell it down in the village? You've got transport?'

'A jeep is transport, ain't it. Ain't going too well though. Army surplus, and I took it as it stood. Never gave much trouble until lately. Plugs just maybe. Points. I don't know a damn.'

Once he began talking he realized he wanted to go on talking. He was a very lonely man. Very independent. Looking into his hard grey eyes, Ames could detect the ghosts of old memories lurking. They lurked because Dobbs would be even lonelier without them. There was something sad about a man in his fifties walking backwards into the future.

'I could have a look at the jeep in the morning,' Ames volunteered.

'Say, you could, could you? You know a little about cars?'

'A little. I could clear a ditch at a pinch, weed a bean row. I'm pretty versatile. I never milked a cow, though.'

'I noticed your hands,' Dobbs said. 'I wondered. City man with callouses. With a healthy outdoor skin like you've got.'

'Well, I've been out of the city for a spell. I stop here for a while, there for a while. I might do a stint with a shovel. I did as a matter of fact at the last place I dropped off.'

'Your business is your own, stranger. All right. We'll see what happens. Make a cash adjustment.'

'For how long?' Ames wondered.

'Don't let's rush it any, mister. Like I said, we'll see what happens.'

* * *

Ames awakened early next morning. Even so he heard Dobbs rustling around down in the kitchen. A wonderful aroma of frying ham was creeping up the stairs.

'You stay outside there until the grub's good and ready, Whitey. And keep your yap shet, understand?'

Pans rattled dimly on the stove. Plates clattered. Ames smelled coffee then. He felt very hungry. He was pulling on his trousers when the door closed and the house went still.

Downstairs, breakfast was keeping warm on the stove. The table was covered with a spotless white cloth, and cup, saucer and dishes, were ready to do service.

Ames put out eggs, ham and golden flapjacks on to plates and sat down with the coffee pot in front of him. When he had eaten he lit a cigarette and went outside into a bright, sunny morning.

There were numerous outhouses round back. The chickens had been turned loose on a wide, fenced run. Ames saw a large bowl of brown and white eggs in the doorway of one of the outhouses. He found Dobbs in another, sitting on a stool and squirting foamy milk into a pail. A huge can belonging to a creamery company stood waiting for the milk.

'Morning, Mr Dobbs.'

'Morning, stranger. You had your breakfast?'

'Sure did. Never had a finer meal anywhere.' Dobbs grunted and said nothing and Ames went on, 'Where do I find the jeep?'

'She's over there on your right. There isn't any hurry.'

'All the same, I'll look it over. Does a truck call for the milk?'

'Yeah, it does. It'll be arriving in half an hour or so.'

Ames went to find the jeep and back it out of the dim shed. There was a box of tools which he opened. He stripped off his jacket and rolled up his sleeves. The sun beat down warmly on his back as he bent over the engine. It didn't take long to find what he guessed to be the trouble. The points had seen their day. The plugs too had done many thousand miles more than their expected performance. He went to join Dobbs who was transferring a pail of milk to the creamery can.

'Points and plugs need replacing,' he said. 'I'll drive into the village and get them. I noticed a service station on the way through.'

'I wouldn't want to put you out of your way, stranger.'

'Forget it. There certainly is a roughness in the engine. If plugs and points don't effect a cure, then we'd better probe further.'

Ames drove down to the village and

bought what he needed at the service station. He bought a newspaper too and set off back to the old farmhouse.

A short time later he started up the jeep engine and listened to it running.

'How does she sound now?'

'Swell,' Dobbs said. 'Like I told you, I'm no dab hand as a motor mechanic.'

'I'll run her up the road and make sure.'

The jeep swept over the hills with the minimum of fuss and Ames returned to the back yard once more. The dog Whitey didn't bark at him now, but lay on the front porch and basked in the early heat.

It was an hour afterwards when the truck arrived to collect the milk. Dobbs talked with the driver for a few minutes. Ames was cleaning his shotgun on the back porch and heard the truck drive off. Then Dobbs came round to him, anxious to talk about something, Ames saw.

'Hank was telling me there was a raid over by Blakeville last night,' Dobbs said. 'Some gang held up a gas station. They coshed the manager so bad they figure he might die. This here country is going to hell with bells on.'

'Oh,' Ames said and laid his rags and oil aside. 'How far from here to Blakeville?'

'Not all that far. Fifty miles or so. Hank said he read about it in the paper. Well, it doesn't take much to make news in these parts.'

Ames remembered his own paper he had brought from Boynton, but he didn't look at it just then. He did later, however, finding an account of the robbery in a centre page.

Service Station Hold-up

'Last evening, at early dusk, a car drove up to Casey's Service Station on the edge of Blakeville. Manager Bill Carson had let his help off duty early and was in sole charge of the station when the car arrived. The driver — whom Carson believes to have been a woman — remained in the car while two men got out of the back. One of them told Carson to fill up whilst his confederate moved in behind him. Carson remembered nothing more until another motorist arrived and brought him round. He was able to ascertain that the till had been robbed of two thousand dollars. In hospital he was conscious for long enough to give the police a brief description. A large-scale search is under way.'

Two men and a woman, Ames thought excitedly. And the robbery had taken place just fifty miles or so away from this very spot. Eve Birchall and two of her friends?

To keep up appearances he took his shotgun down to the lake that afternoon. Dobbs had kept putting off talking about money, but Ames insisted he accept fifty dollars as a token of his good will. At sight of the money Dobbs' face had lit up and any reservations he might have been harbouring concerning his visitor appeared to vanish.

So far Ames hadn't referred to any other visitors that the man might have had during the past months. The house had been empty when he'd bought it, he had explained to Ames. He had no idea of who had lived there before him.

It was the following day, when the morning chores were over and the creamery truck had gone, that Ames broached this subject. He realized that he might waste a lot of time at the farmhouse if none of the gang ever called to make a check regarding a contact from Mel Savage. Privately Ames thought it very unlikely that any of the gang would dare visit when there was a new owner in residence. He was willing to wait for a month, of course, as Savage had indicated he should. But if the gang had moved closer to Blakeville than they had to their former hideout, it might pay him to make a trip to the locality on the off-chance of catching a whisper concerning Eve or her friends.

'Callers?' Dobbs repeated when Ames mentioned if he ever had any. 'Staying here like you, you mean?'

'Don't think I'm getting curious, Mr Dobbs,' Ames said casually and laughed.

'Hey, you ain't talking about dames? What in hell would a dame see in an old gopher like me?'

'What gave you this notion you're an

old gopher? You're not that old. You look to be in your prime. Shave off those whiskers and you'd come through as a reasonably handsome buck.'

It was Dobbs' turn to laugh, and he laughed until tears came to his eyes.

'I ain't got no time for dames,' he chuckled presently. 'I was married to one good woman, mister. She upped and died on me, and that was that.'

'I'm sorry to hear about it, Mr Dobbs.'

'Funny you should bring it up, though,' the man continued slowly. 'About a woman calling, I mean. About every four or five weeks, I guess, a woman does happen by here. Pretty too in a way, if you go for her sort.'

'She calls at your house?'

'Yeah, she does. I used to think she had a trailer parked someplace in this neck of the woods. But I travelled around a little — just to satisfy a whim, you understand. I never did see any trailer.'

'Could be she comes from one of the other farms hereabouts?'

'Buying eggs?'

'Eggs?' Ames murmured and hoped he

didn't look too tense. 'Oh, I see what you're driving at. She calls here to buy eggs?'

'That's right. She's always polite. Always asks me how I'm getting on. I asked her in one time to have a drink of coffee if she felt like it. She just said thanks and no.'

'You've got something at least to look forward to. Expect she'll be calling for eggs one of these days pretty soon.'

'I wouldn't care to bet on it, mister. Two months have gone now and I haven't seen her. Reckon she's getting bigger eggs elsewhere, or she's getting them cheaper.'

5

The news provided fresh stimulus for Ames' enthusiasm. A woman who made periodic calls at the farmhouse to buy eggs. A woman who was pretty in a way. She came out of nowhere and went back to nowhere, for all Dobbs knew.

Ames let the subject drop so as not to arouse suspicion in the older man. The woman just had to be Eve Birchall. If this was so, then it meant that Mel Savage had been right about her. She was living in the hope that, somehow or other, Mel would think of some move, devise some plan that would eventually pave the way for them getting together again to share the proceeds of the bank robbery.

If she was the woman of the gas station holdup at Blakeville it indicated her rigidity of purpose, her iron determination that the quarter million should stay hidden until the gang leader was free and in a position to reassert himself. To make ends meet the gang must be indulging in whatever small-time stuff that came to hand.

This triggered off an itching curiosity in Ames to make contact with Eve Birchall as soon as possible. There seemed no doubt of her being a woman out of the ordinary run. Such a woman would be patient and will herself to be self-sufficient. She would form her own ideas and ideals and hold fast to them with all the tenacity she possessed.

In the morning Ames made the excuse of wanting to buy a paper to go off to Boynton again. Dobbs looked at him with a faint sneer tugging at his mouth.

'Reckon you must be fooling yourself, stranger,' he said.

'Howcome, Mr Dobbs?'

'You kid yourself you want to take a break away from society, while it keeps drawing you like a magnet until you can't resist the need.'

Ames laughed gruffly.

'You know, oldtimer, you're a lot sharper than a man would take you for.'

‘I’m sharp enough, I reckon. I get by. I’ve got a radio there I haven’t listened to in months. As for newspapers — well, what the hell sense is there in buying newspapers? What’s news today is history tomorrow. In three-four days it’s dead and forgotten. The world goes on just the same as if nobody had said a word, doesn’t it?’

‘You may have got a point, Mr Dobbs.’

‘Quit calling me Mr Dobbs, will you. My name is Jack. Anything wrong with calling me Jack?’

‘Okay, Jack. But quit calling me stranger, will you. My name is Lew.’

Dobbs relented to the extent of giving a brief rasping laugh that started the dog on the front porch barking.

Ames drove into Boynton and bought cigarettes and a newspaper. He also bought another dozen cans of beer. Despite Dobbs’ offhand regard for beer, Ames had discovered he liked it well enough.

Back at the car he scanned through the paper for further news of the gas station holdup. Today the incident rated only a short paragraph. The police were still searching for the robbers, but as yet had made no arrests. Bill Carson, the manager, had regained consciousness and there were now hopes of his being able to make a recovery. 'No thanks to these ruthless thugs', the writer appended.

Leaving his purchases in the car, Ames went into a pay phone and put a call through to Delton City. A short time later he was speaking with Edward Ogden. He told his chief what had developed to date and said it was his belief that the woman who bought eggs from Dobbs was none other than Eve Birchall.

'It's a reasonable assumption to make, Lew. You could be right. But, as the hill-billy says, it's a long time since she last called.'

'I'll hang on anyhow, sir.'

'Of course. But, Lew, there was another angle to this that I spent quite a while considering. I refrained from mentioning it to you until you made a real break. Let's say this woman is the one you want to contact. It would then mean that you have the key to the quarter million dollars. Right?'

'I get it,' Ames said slowly. 'But don't forget that the key is split into two parts. The woman has one piece and her boyfriend has the other. To make music the parts must come together.'

'I know, Lew. And here is my point. The process, if left to the individuals concerned, could be a prolonged and painful one. Why not cut it short?'

'Arrange to make it casy for the boyfriend?'

'Work it out for yourself, Lew. You hold a dominating position. When the two get together the truth will come to light. After that it would simply be a case of moving in rapidly.'

Ames cursed softly under his breath.

'What's that you say?'

'Nothing. Look, chief, take my word for it, it wouldn't work. We're dealing with a sophisticated team. A false note would ruin the whole symphony. Will you allow me to go ahead?'

'I'm leaving it to you,' Edward Ogden agreed. 'All I'd offer you at this juncture is advice.'

'I'm exceedingly grateful, sir. I'll keep in touch when I can. But there could be deep silences.'

'Fully understood. Over and out, Lew.'

'Goodbye, sir.'

Ames got into the Dodge and drove back to Dobbs' farm.

He was planning on another visit to the lake to pass the time when they heard a car jar to a halt outside and Whitey went into a shrill barking.

'Somebody coming a-visiting, looks like, Jack.'

'Odd,' the older man muttered and hurried through the kitchen to reach the front door.

Ames stood at the window where he could see over the front yard. The inner door slammed and Whitey gave a pained yelp before subsiding into silence. The car was a dust-streaked sedan, and it wasn't a woman who dismounted, as Ames fondly hoped it would be, but a rugged looking man in cord trousers and rain-breaker jacket. Ames' stomach lumped when he spotted the badge glinting in the sunshine. He heard clearly what they said.

'How're the cows milking these days, Jack?'

'Fair to middling, Sheriff,' Dobbs said. 'Another bunch of hippies broke loose in the district?'

'Nothing like that,' the sheriff responded. 'You heard about the Blakeville robbery, maybe?'

'Yeah, I did. Hank told me first of all, and then Lew read about it in the paper.'

'Lew is a new partner you've taken on?'

Dobbs gave a laugh that sounded like a cackle to Ames' ears. The sheriff was looking straight at the window now.

'When did I ever have a partner, Sheriff? No, this is a strange fella that passed by. He's putting up here for a few days. City man. Getting in some breathing for a change. Doing a little shooting.'

'Is he here now?'

'Sure. Come ahead in and say hello.'

Ames knew what was on the sheriff's mind, although Dobbs didn't appear to have grasped it yet. The sheriff came in and shook hands with Ames. He had brown eyes crinkled at the corners, and chewed gum vigorously. He regarded Ames closely.

'Just routine, Mr Ames,' he said. 'I got a wire to do a little checking around. Somebody said Jack had got a partner or a lodger.'

'Must have been Hank,' Dobbs said. 'You can't piss but somebody wants to talk about it.'

'Where were you night before last, Mr Ames?' the sheriff said.

'He was right here,' Dobbs answered him. 'Hey, you're not trying to rope him in for what happened over in Blakeville, by any chance, Sherriff?'

'I'm speaking to Mr Ames, Jack. You can have your say afterwards. What about it, Ames?'

'Jack is right anyhow,' Ames replied. 'I drove through Boynton around sundown. I reached Jack's place at dusk.'

'You didn't go out again?'

Ames shook his head.

'How about it, Jack?' the sheriff said to the pent-up Dobbs. 'Can you verify what he says?'

'What the hell you think I just done?'

Dobbs demanded. 'He got here about dark. He never left the house again.'

'You could check out my story in the village. The attendant at the station will remember me.'

'I've already done that,' the lawman responded. 'Like I said, I was just checking.' A wide grin split his features. 'No offence, I hope?'

'Of course not,' Ames said. 'You've got your job to do.'

'Planning to stay long in these parts, Mr Ames?'

'A few days. Maybe a month if Jack can stand me. I come in handy when the jeep misfires.'

The sheriff shared his chuckle. Dobbs just stared as though the doubting of his word was a serious affront.

'Want a cup of java?' he invited meagrely.

'No, thanks, Jack. I'd better be about my business. The way I figure it, the gang that made the gas station grab will have high-tailed it long since. So-long, you guys.'

The sheriff went on out to his car and

Ames followed him. 'The gas station holdup an isolated incident?' he inquired.
'You could say so. For these parts. It's a peaceful neck of the woods. That doesn't say you mustn't maintain a constant vigilance. Be seeing you, Mr Ames.'
'Sure, Sheriff.'

* * *

A week went past at the Dobbs farm, and another. Daily Ames grew less hopeful of Eve Birchall ever turning up here again. The woman had practised being faithful and patient, but even virtues have their limitations, and she couldn't be expected to hold on until she had fallen arches and grey hair.

The big question that rose to Ames' mind was: what course would Evelyn Birchall take on the day she decided she was living in a cocoon shaped of dreams, and that Mel Savage was fated to serve out his time in prison? Would she strive to initiate a plan for the springing of Savage, or would she endeavour to forget him and latch on with some other man?

He looked at it from a different angle, from the angle, in fact, that Mel Savage himself viewed the wider canvas. Savage had declared that Eve's act of taking off with the quarter million and hiding it had been motivated by her intention of talking the remaining members of the gang into staging an escape bid for him. But a lot of time had passed and Savage was still in prison. Which seemed to point to the woman's original plans having gone awry. Did this leave her with nothing but the hope that Mel himself would come up with a bright idea, and that sooner or later he would discover some method of transmitting the idea to her? Had she finally discarded all hope of ever being reunited with him?

Considering all the possibilities leading out from this conclusion, Ames was forced to face up to the reality of his own efforts being so much wastage of time and manpower.

It might have been better to revise the entire *modus operandi*, which would have entailed the framing of an escape for Savage, and then following him wherever he went. But, as Ames had already deduced and pointed out to the chief, Savage was nobody's fool and would be the first person to smell a rat. Better then to bet on a long chance than to have the entire thing freeze up on them?

There was only one logical answer to that one.

Thus Ames told himself he was working in the most sensible and acceptable pattern.

* * *

He had been at the farm for sixteen days when the cogs meshed and clicked out the sort of rhythm he had been waiting for.

It was wearing to noon, and he had returned from a shooting session down at Looking Glass Lake, when a car drove up the track to the house and the horn was sounded, sending Whitey into a spasm of frantic barking.

'Well, what d'you know!' Dobbs cried as he headed for the front door. 'That's her. That's the dame who calls to buy eggs. She always blows her horn when she arrives.'

'She never comes in?' Ames queried, moving over to the window.

'Never,' Dobbs told him. 'I guess she's scared I'll try and take a bite out of her one day. Come on out, Lew, and say hello.'

'No, I'll not, Jack. If she's as sensitive as you say she is I might scare your customer off.'

'Suit yourself,' Dobbs chuckled and went on out to the sunshine.

From the window Ames had a pretty clear view of the car and the woman sitting behind the steering wheel. She was darkhaired, he saw, with a sharply-cut profile. When she turned her face to the oncoming Dobbs the rather pale features relaxed in a faint smile.

'Well, howdy there, ma'am!' Dobbs greeted. 'Figured you had drifted on out of the country.'

Ames couldn't hear what she said in return. They held a lengthy conversation, Dobbs doing most of the talking and wagging his head occasionally. He wondered if he ought to go out and show himself to the girl. But no. The shock of seeing someone else at the farm might throw a fright in her. He would play it cool. His mind buzzed with the nucleus of a plan of approach.

At last Dobbs left her, carrying a basket for the eggs. He didn't come through the house but went on round to the back. The woman brought a compact from her purse and started powdering her nose. Suddenly her gaze fell on the Dodge in the front yard and he watched her eyes widen and then narrow.

She switched her attention to the window and Ames stepped back to be beyond her line of vision. Even so he could still follow the shades of expression she registered. She was both curious and apprehensive. Perhaps she wondered if the police had succeeded in tracing the Maytown bank robbers to the farm, where they had planned the robbery, and where the police might pick up clues.

A twist of her head told him that Dobbs was returning from the rear of the building. The basket was laden now and he opened the back door of the car to place it on the seat. Money was passed over. Dobbs wanted to delay her, but the girl had other ideas. She took the car through the entrance gateway, reversed, and drove off down the track.

Dobbs was walking towards the front porch where Whitey was barking once more when Ames dashed to the rear of the house and emerged on the yard. He walked briskly to the front, and was stooping at the gateway as Dobbs came out.

'I wondered where the devil you'd gone, Lew,' he said. 'Hey, what's up?'

'The dame must have dropped this, Jack.' Ames straightened and extended a bill.'

'Did she now? I didn't notice. How much?'

'Five dollars. It might be a lot of money to her.'

'Yeah, it might. Look, I could catch her, maybe.'

'My car's handy,' Ames said. He pushed the bill into his pocket and headed for the Dodge.'

'Want me to go with you? She might

think it funny as I didn't tell her anybody was here.'

'Don't worry. I'll explain.'

Ames slammed the car door shut and gunned the engine to life. He cut out of the yard and bounced off along the uneven track. At the road junction he was in time to see the woman's dark green Ford surmount a rise and vanish in a billow of dust. She was driving in the direction opposite to Boynton and Ames surged after her.

He was glad he had made certain of the Dodge having a good engine. Coming over the crest of the hill where the Ford had disappeared, he saw it a long way off, boiling over a stretch of open country.

It soon became evident that Eve Birchall — as she must be Eve Birchall, Ames reasoned — had seen his car in her driving mirror and had formed the worst conclusion. He was a cop who had traced the gang this far and was hunting for a lead.

Mile after mile rushed past in clouds of thick, yellowish dust. Ames was gradually gaining on the Ford, and he hoped the woman would not get excited to the point of sheer recklessness.

The road climbed another long, punishing hill. The Ford was surging up it at full tilt, but even so the Dodge was gaining ground rapidly. Over the hill a section of woodland lay ahead. The Ford swung into a bend and slithered practically into the trees. It righted itself and raced from Ames' sight. Now Ames really tramped the gas pedal to the board. It would be rank bad luck if the woman wrecked the car and killed herself in her fright.

He had another glimpse of her where the trees reached out over the road to form a dusky, dust-shrouded tunnel. Then he was on another straight and there was no sign of the car in front of him.

Suspecting what had happened, Ames went for the brakes. He had difficulty in reversing on the narrow track and was forced to mount the soft shoulder where tree trunks were rooted. Finally he made it and cruised back the way he had come.

He braked harshly when he saw the

Ford's hood reflecting the sunlight that filtered down through the tall branches. His first thought was that the woman would have taken off on foot. But he was wrong. She had driven in amongst the trees and alighted.

Leaping out of the Dodge he saw a movement at the back of the car. Then a pale, big-eyed face showed, and a hand came up to point at him. Clutched firmly in the fingers was a gun.

'Don't come a step closer,' the woman warned in a tense husky voice. 'If you do I will shoot.'

6

She was the kind of woman that Ames thought of as full-blown; he knew this was just another way of saying mature, but mature lacked the connotations of experience, awareness and sensuality he wished to attribute here. Eve Birchall had all these qualities and then some. She would be about twenty-eight, he judged. Her hair really was dark — a blue-black that caught the vagrant bars of sunlight slanting through the trees and reflected them in glossy sheen. She stood tall for a woman — five feet, seven, at least, with a straight body that was wide-hipped and full-breasted, and challenging in every line of its utter femininity.

She was wearing a sensible linen skirt, and jacket to match that was buttoned across a fine sweater. The eyes that regarded him were fearless and determined. The word moll sprang to Ames' mind too, but he rejected it as trite and almost meaningless in the context.

The cheekbones were delicately constructed to the point of fragility, and there were little hollows in the cheeks themselves which Ames found oddly disturbing. The mouth was both sensual and petulant, and at that moment the aura surrounding her was of outright defiance.

'You've got it all wrong,' he said carefully, deciding she might be desperate enough underneath the hard poise to squeeze the trigger of the gun she held. 'I'm not a cop.'

'It doesn't matter to me what you are,' she replied in a controlled voice. 'You were following me. You were bent on overtaking me, and that is enough.'

'For what?' he said and laughed shortly. 'Shooting me? Drawing a gun on me, even? Shoot me and you'd be making the greatest mistake of your life, Eve.'

His use of her name had an electrifying effect on her. She jerked and the dark eyes blazed like those of an animal at bay.

'How do you know my name?' she snapped hoarsely.

'So it really is your name?'

'I don't know what you're talking about. I've warned you, mister. Take another step. Make a false move of any description. I'll shoot you if you do.'

'You're Eve Birchall, aren't you? If you are, then for pete's sake say that you are. I don't want to waste any more time in following a bum trail.'

The rougher manner adopted by Ames tended to throw the girl slightly off balance. The gun wavered momentarily, but then steaded while the lips firmed in on themselves.

'Perhaps you'd better explain,' she suggested grimly.

'My name is Ames.'

'It could be King Kong for all I know or care. Is that clear? I saw your car parked at Dobbs' farm. But it doesn't give you the right to light after me like a bat out of hell. I nearly crashed, if you don't know.'

'I figured that you might if you weren't careful. It would have been a powerful loss of woman to the world, not to mention the scenery you could have spoiled.'

'Listen, mister, I'm growing kind of tired of your iron nerve and your soft patter. If you've got anything to say to me, then say it.'

'Okay. I will. But first of all, wouldn't it be wise if you took your car out of that tangle? A patrol cop happens by, he'll ask you more questions than I could dream up.'

She thought this over for a moment. It worried her. She teetered on the brink of indecision.

'All right,' Ames said. 'You fear a trick. I'll show you I'm not in the mood for tricks today. I'll drive your car back to the road.'

'No,' she said sharply, her distrust reasserting itself. 'I can manage myself.'

'Make it snappy. But don't take off. And remember you'll have to shift your gun away from my face.'

'You do it then,' she said quickly. 'Go on. And you try any gags with my car and I'll let you have it before you get very far.'

'Baby, when you get to know me better you'll realize I'd never pull a fast one on a dame who had me covered with a gun.

You are so goddamned jumpy.'

So saying, Ames went to the Ford and started the engine. The girl stepped back swiftly when the front wheels dropped into a hole and the car took a sudden pitch towards her. Ames fought with the steering and sent it lurching to the road. He drove the front of the car close to the front of the Dodge, set the parking brake and got out. The girl had followed him to the road and continued to level the gun at him.

'Let's sit in your car while we talk,' Ames said.

'No go, mister. You're pretty strong on this talk stuff. When are you going to get it off your chest?'

Ames was reaching for his cigarettes when she told him to freeze. The bleakness in the husky voice compelled him to do exactly that.

'You're so keen on sitting while you talk,' she said. 'All right. Get on to the front seat of my car. I'll sit in behind you and listen.'

'But — '

'I'm telling you, funny man.'

Shrugging, Ames did as she ordered, splaying his fingers over the steering wheel. The girl got in back and slammed the door after her. A second later Ames felt the cold outline of the gun muzzle against his neck.

'Now talk,' she breathed icily.

'Once upon a time there were three bears — '

'Cut it out, you lousy creep! I'm sick and tired of your fancy act. Who are you, and what do you want with me?'

'Are you Evelyn Birchall?'

'Here we go again!'

The muzzle of the gun bit into the flesh of Ames' neck.

'You must tell me,' he panted. 'You are or you're not. I've got to know what I'm doing, haven't I.'

'I'm Eve Birchall. So what? Your name is Ames. Again, so what? You were stopping there at Dobbs' place. And again, so what?'

'Simmer down, Eve. I've got an item in my pocket you'd better have a hard gander at.'

'Sure!' she sneered. 'A gun of your

own. Or would it be a knife?'

'I'm not armed.'

'You're armed plenty, mister. With enough nerve to take you through a wall of rock. What's this thing you want me to look at?'

'A note.'

Followed a moment of heavy silence. Then, in a more downbeat tone, 'A note? What sort of note?'

'From your boyfriend, Eve.'

'You fancy-pants smartaleck! I haven't got a boyfriend. You're pulling a tall bluff.'

'His name is Mel Savage.'

'You're a brass-necked liar,' she almost moaned. 'How do I happen to be tied up with anyone called Savage?'

'I could tell you that too, baby. All of it. Only it's a hell of a drawn-out story, and it might take until midnight to spell it out for you in the right language. In the meantime, Dobbs is thinking I drove after you to return a five-dollar bill you dropped at the gateway.'

'I didn't drop any bill at the gateway.'

'I said you had and Dobbs believed me.

If I don't get back there soon, Dobbs is going to wonder if I was pulling his leg.'

'It was an excuse to follow me?'

'I thought it was a pretty good one. I had to dream up something that wouldn't arouse his curiosity, hadn't I?'

'I don't know anybody called Mel Savage.'

'Okay, okay. Don't make a scene out of it. But you can read the note all the same. It won't hurt you that much.'

'Which pocket is it in?'

'My inner jacket one. You'll have to move up to me real close if you want to remove it yourself.'

'You remove it, mister. But do it carefully. I can handle this gun with the best of them.'

'I'd be the last person to doubt your word, honey.'

'Shove that honey-baby stuff if you don't mind. Produce the note. But I still say you're cuckoo.'

Ames extracted the note he had hidden deep down in the pocket and passed it over his shoulder.

'Can I light a cigarette now?'

'If you make one small move I'll blow your brains out.'

Ames listened carefully for her reaction. She didn't disappoint him. He heard a swift hissing intake of breath. Then the bore of the gun pressed even deeper into his neck.

'Where did you get this?' she cried tremulously.

'Look, doll, what about growing up and getting wise? Where do you imagine I got it?

'I can't say where you got it, mister. I told you I don't know Mel Savage.'

'You're a liar, Eve. A fetching one I won't deny, but a liar all the same. That or you aren't Eve Birchall at all. That came from Mel in a prison farm. Maybe you never heard he'd been transferred to a prison farm. Well, he was. I'm one guy can tell you so for a fact. I was there myself until a few weeks ago.'

'Where have you been since?' she asked tautly, doubt and suspicion making her voice thick.

'Staying with Dobbs. Go ask him if you want to check.'

'You can see me doing that. Why were you staying with him?'

'We were having an affair. Look, why did you keep calling there for eggs? Hoping you'd find a chicken in one some day?'

'I wanted to — '

She stopped speaking abruptly. In a moment she released the pressure of the gun against Ames' neck. Ames turned his head and stared at her. He could see she was fighting a battle with herself.

'Let me tell you why you kept calling, Eve. It was the last place you had contact with Mel before you set out for Maytown and the bank there. You had the idea at the back of your mind that if Mel was ever to renew the contract he would use your old hideaway as a stepping stone.'

'You're making wild guesses, mister. You're still talking moonshine as far as I'm concerned.'

'Oh, no I'm not, honey. I'm getting through to where you live with every word I say. Let me go on from there. Why was I staying with Dobbs? I didn't know Dobbs would be at that house. Mel didn't allow for the eventuality. But I had to make the most of it, hadn't I? I promised to help your boyfriend. He gave me the note. Could you figure out how much effort and risk went into the writing of the note, the smuggling of it from the prison camp?'

'You must have had a real ball,' she said with affected carelessness.

'If you want to believe so, then Mel is still having a ball. You read what he wrote. You recognized his writing. He asked you to trust me.'

'He asked me to trust a Lew Ames.'

'So where's the problem? I'm Lew Ames.'

'You say you are. You could be Billy the Kid for all I could ever guess.'

'Driving licence?'

She refused to respond to this. She merely kept looking at him. Ames produced his wallet from his pocket and handed over the driving licence.

'You live in Delton City. Lots of bright lights, I hear.'

'For some folks it's a paradise, no doubt. For a guy who started off as a door-to-door salesman and graduated to the pen it isn't such a steam.'

'What did they lock you up for — breaking into kiddies' piggy banks?'

'Sneer all you feel like, baby. It runs off me the way water runs off a duck's feathers. A duck's feathers pack some kind of grease. It's what I've accumulated since then. I got drunk and knocked down a pedestrian. At my trial he was referred to as an innocent citizen. In my book he was a jerkwater jaywalker.'

'He died?'

'He sure turned up his toes and laid off breathing for long enough to be put into a hole in the ground.'

'Excuse me while I weep a bucketful of tears for you.'

She handed him back his licence. She continued to look at him steadily.

'All right,' Ames shrugged. 'I've tried to assist your boyfriend, but you don't really want him back in circulation. You're having too good a time with some young stud, I bet.'

She slashed the back of her free hand across his face. Her eyes blazed with a stormy anger.

‘Shut your dirty mouth,’ she panted. ‘For two pins I’d pull this trigger and leave you here for the cops to find.’

‘Go on and do it if the pressure’s so high,’ Ames taunted. ‘You’re sufficiently hardboiled to kill a man. How many notches have you grooved out so far?’

‘I’m telling you, smart guy!’

‘Sure, sure. You’re telling me. You’ve told me. Back up, will you. I’m getting out of this heap and going back to my own heap. Then I’m going to build me a rag doll — just like you — and stick a thousand pins into the damn thing.’

‘What’s in it for you?’

‘Come again, rag doll.’

‘How much were you promised to do what you’re doing?’ she almost shouted.

‘Calm down. Don’t blow your cool. Mel promised me a hundred grand for my good deed.’

‘That explains it!’

‘Why shouldn’t it explain it? I’m a mean, tight-fisted guy with a mercenary soul. I happen to like dough. Who doesn’t like dough? Are you telling me you put your nose in the air every time you hear two C-bills making love?'

Ames stretched his hand to the door of the car and opened it. When he smiled coldly down at the woman she was sitting with the gun on her lap. Her face reflected only a fraction of the turmoil raging in her.

Ames stepped out to the road.

'Wait.'

'I'm waiting,' he said, taking note of the smoothly rounded knees, the full curve of thigh. A vein throbbed in her throat.

'Are you staying with Dobbs for much longer?'

'No longer than it takes me to pack my duffle. Why are you interested?'

'And you want to go on with this?'

'I'm not so sure. I'm used to a certain amount of scepticism and opposition, but I haven't got any use for a sour deal. No matter how attractive,' he added with an inflection that sent dark colour mounting briefly in her pale cheeks.

'The decision isn't mine alone to make.'

'Mel explained. There are four of you. Three men and a woman. The woman's name is Eve Birchall. The names of the men are, Art Macklin, Dave Huggins and Milo Farland.'

'I'll have to see them, talk with them.'

'You do that, Eve. In the meantime think of your boyfriend using a pickaxe on rocks. Think of the sweat he's losing. Think of the way he's thinking of you.'

'Stop it!'

'Goodbye, Eve.'

Ames started round to his own car. She yelled after him. 'Come back.'

'Yeah?' he said wearily when he returned to lean on the window ledge.

'Did — did he have a plan?'

'I have the plan. I figured it might be worth a hundred thousand peanuts to me. But it isn't. So what do I not do? I don't cry over spilt milk.'

'All right,' she said quickly. 'I'm not saying I trust you entirely. I'm not saying my friends will trust you either. But I'll put it to them.'

'And then?'

'Where can I get in touch with you again? If you stayed with Dobbs — '

'Sorry. Dobbs and I are beginning to

grow on each other. I've got itchy feet and I'm going to drift.'

'Do you know how to get to Parkdale?'

'It's a town, isn't it?'

'It's a hundred miles to the east of here. There is a small hotel on Cooper Street. Will you go there, book into a room, and wait?'

'For how long? I've been waiting around since I got out of that prison farm.'

'Not for long,' she said, yielding momentarily to the eagerness that was gripping her.

'Why can't I take off with you now?' Ames queried.

'You can't. As I've explained, this isn't only just me. There are others involved. Others to be considered.'

'Could you give me a date?'

'This is Wednesday. Make it Monday next at the outside. If I don't call with you, one of my friends will.'

Ames lifted his shoulders and grinned meagrely.

'What have I got to lose? They say that what you never had you never miss. Okay,

Eve, you've got yourself a bargain.'

He extended his hand for her to meet. She began to stretch out her own hand but drew it back.

'Until Monday, mister,' she said coldly.

Ames got into his car, reversed a little to give him room to manoeuvre. Driving off into the direction of Dobbs' place he waved a salute.

The picture he took away with him was of dark, staring eyes in a pale blank face.

7

In the late afternoon he decided to drive into Boynton once more. There was no telephone at Dobbs', and he wished to apprise Edward Ogden of the latest events.

Before leaving he mentioned casually to Dobbs that he was thinking of moving on shortly. Dobbs had become so used to him around the house that he refused to comprehend for a few seconds.

'Leave for where, Lew?' he said. 'And when are you coming back again?'

'You miss the point,' Ames smiled. 'It's time I was returning to my work in the city. To live a man must eat, oldtimer; to eat it's necessary to work. Pretty horrible setup, I know, but I didn't invent it.'

'I'll sure miss you, Lew.'

'Same here, Jack. I'll probably drive through the hills once in a while to say howdy.'

'When are you going to drift?' Dobbs

said, a lugubrious expression on his face.

The query caused Ames to set a definite day for his departure.

'Early on Friday. It'll give me the weekend to straighten myself out.'

Dobbs said nothing for a moment, then he shrugged philosophically.

'Suppose I'll have to get back on speaking terms with Whitey,' he cackled.

Ames drove into the village and put a call through for Edward Ogden. The chief sounded surprised to hear he had made contact with Eve Birchall.

'Well, well, Lew. You never really know with women, do you now?'

'You're as well equipped as I am to answer that, sir. She certainly is a tough proposition, and if she's representative of her friends, then I'm really going to enjoy myself.'

'How about laying on another man to help?'

'As I see it, it wouldn't be advisable. It's strictly a chore for a loner. That prison farm gave me lots of practice.'

'You think they'll go ahead and endeavour to spring the party? If they do and you can let me know, we could make arrangements for an abortion.'

'I wouldn't trust anyone at the prison farm with a harmless rumour. I'd rather allow events to take their natural course.'

Ames spoke for another few minutes with his chief, then he said goodbye and hung up.

On Friday morning, directly after breakfast was over, he forced another fifty dollars on Dobbs, shook the man's gnarled hand, and drove off through the hills.

It was afternoon before he reached Parkdale. The delay had been caused by a back wheel blowout, and when he'd started to change the wheel he discovered the jack was faulty. But he was in no hurry, he told himself. He had until Monday before anyone from Eve would show up looking for him.

Parkdale lay roughly to the east of Boynton and was a town about half the size of Delton City. A half-hour after arriving he found Cooper Street and the small fleapit hotel he'd been told to book into.

A hard rain was beginning to fall as he left the car and entered the hotel lobby. Some people had edged in off the street and he had to push through them to gain the desk. While he waited for the clerk to sort through a bundle of envelopes he let his gaze run idly over the lobby. The man in charge of the news-stand was immersed in a magazine. A fat man had come in behind Ames. He sat down on a basket chair, placed a cigar between his teeth, and began leafing at a newspaper.

'Yes, sir. What can I do for you?'

Ames turned to face the middle-aged clerk. He had brown hair receding rapidly at the temples. The fixed smile contrived painlessly by lifting his lips from his teeth and narrowing his eyes a little was the product of many years of practice. He had ceased being genuinely interested in people and now he simply made a pretence of being interested. He had seen all there was to see and nothing would ever excite him.

'I'd like a room,' Ames told him. 'I don't expect the last word in luxury, but I don't wish to go wildly primitive either.'

It ran off the desk clerk much as the rain was running off the deserted sidewalk.

'I've got the very thing for you, sir,' he said equably. 'On the third floor.' He squinted appraisingly at the battered suitcase which Ames was straddling. 'How long will you be staying?'

'About a week,' I guess.

He mentioned a rate which Ames agreed to. Then he thumped a bell on the desk and an ancient bellboy emerged from a doorway, grinding a cigarette stub under his foot before moving forward. He waited while Ames signed the register.

'Show this gentleman to three-one-two. I hope you'll find everything to your liking, sir.' The cliché came out with the mechanical emotion of a computer.

They rode to the third floor in the self service elevator. The bellhop opened the door and gestured Ames through, then carried in the suitcase. He went to the window and opened the blinds, then pried in the bedroom and closet. He came back to smile thinly at Ames. Ames gave him a dollar.

'There's a fat guy sitting down in the lobby,' he said. 'D'you know who he is?'

'I can't say that I even noticed him, sir.'

'It doesn't matter.'

'I'll be back in a few minutes, sir,' the bellboy said and winked.

He was back in five minutes, tapping on the room door as Ames was making his own examination of the squalid quarters. Ames let him in.

'There is no fat man in the lobby.'

'Thanks. Forget it. I was to meet somebody here. He might have gone for a walk in the rain. He might have gone to his room. It doesn't matter.'

The bellhop wasn't finished. 'There is no fat man staying at the hotel,' he told Ames.

'Oh.' Ames smiled. I've got fat men in front of my eyes. Just forget it, will you?'

'Sure. Nothing else at the moment, sir?'

'If I think of anything I'll ring. Thanks.'

He pushed the man in the lobby from his mind. Eve Birchall had said Monday and she would mean Monday. So if she hadn't sent the fat man to the hotel to watch for him, then there was nothing to worry about.

He freshened up and changed his suit, then left the hotel and found a good restaurant where he had a decent meal. The rain had slackened as he left the restaurant.

He drove around Parkdale in the Dodge, halting occasionally to stretch his legs and have a closer look at the sights. In the evening, boredom drove him to a movie theatre where a Western was showing. It was a John Wayne oldie and he thoroughly enjoyed it, even though he had seen it twice before. He enjoyed Western movies, and especially the ones featuring John Wayne.

He was leaving the theatre when he saw the fat man walking across the foyer in front of him. He disappeared in the crowd and Ames hurried after him to the street. There was a Chinese place close to the theatre and a lot of the movie-goers were gravitating towards it.

Ames almost walked into the man in the shadows. He had his back to the cinema wall and was in the process of striking a match to light a cigar. Ames had a glimpse of heavy jowls and a massive forehead under the hat he was wearing. The man didn't even glance at him as Ames caught his balance and moved on.

He walked to the car park where the Dodge was sitting and opened the door to slide under the wheel. If the fat man was looking for an opportunity to speak to him, then he was ready to oblige.

Eve was a smarter woman than he'd taken her for. She had made allowances for his arriving in Parkdale earlier than the day stipulated. She had sent the fat man to the hotel to await his arrival there, and to keep an eye on him until Monday.

This conclusion triggered off slight annoyance in Ames. But what could he expect when he was cruising in the same ship with a gang of hoods. He was a valuable item to them, and as such they saw him as something to be kept under surveillance.

Ten minutes passed and the fat man failed to show up. It meant he was in no way eager to have a word with Ames. His orders were to watch where he went, and what he did, and nothing else.

To satisfy his own curiosity, Ames left the car and walked back to the street. There was no sign of the fat man in the vicinity. It didn't mean he wasn't there; it just meant he had decided to be a less conspicious shadow.

On reflection Ames was glad he had taken heed of the fat man in the hotel lobby. At least he now knew where he stood, and he wouldn't dare communicate with Edward Ogden in case he was asked later to explain whom he had been calling.

Next day was Saturday and he went to a ball game at a local stadium. He kept watching for the fat man, without success. In the evening he ate out at the same restaurant he had visited previously, did another movie — this one a musical — and arrived back at his hotel around midnight.

Sunday it rained for most of the day, and Ames bought a batch of papers and spent the day in his room reading them. Monday dawned with clear skies and the promise of more heat. Ames didn't stray far from the environs of the hotel. He had no idea when the connection would be made, but he wanted to be ready when the fat man struck. He was reasonably sure it would be he who would make the contact.

It was early evening and the daylight was mellowing to a balmy dusk when the telephone in Ames' room rang.

'Yeah. What is it?'

'There is a gentleman here wishing to see you, Mr Ames. He says he would like to go up.'

'What is his name?'

There was a hesitation and then the clerk answered.

'A Mr Mack. He says he is a friend of yours and you're expecting him.'

'That's right, I am. Let him come on up.'

A short time later the door was rapped and Ames opened it to reveal a compactly-built man in a dark suit and narrow-brimmed hat. He was about thirty, Ames would have guessed, with a square jaw, a wide forehead, and cool blue eyes that raced over Ames from the feet up.

'I'm Mr Mack,' he introduced himself. He pushed past Ames without waiting to be asked in. 'I believe you're a Mr Ames?'

'My name is Lew Ames. And yours is Macklin, isn't it?'

'That's so,' the other said. He brought a cigarette pack from the pocket of his jacket and threw one up high enough to catch between his lips. 'Have you got a light?'

'Sure.' Ames half turned to lift his lighter from the table. He had no warning of what was about to happen next.

A hard fist took him low down in the stomach and sent him rocking over a chair to land on the floor on his hands and knees. He winced and shook his head and when he raised it Macklin was sitting on a chair with a .38 Smith and Wesson grasped loosely in his right hand.

'What the hell's the big idea?' Ames rasped from a thick throat. He pushed himself upright, still feeling the effects of the blow despite the layer of tough muscle he had cultivated.

'You tell me, chum,' Macklin said. He pushed his hat up from his forehead with the muzzle of the gun, felt in his pocket for a lighter and flipped it beneath his cigarette. He blew smoke at Ames.

'I don't get it. I don't understand. You said that you were Macklin.'

'And you said you were Lew Ames.'

'I am Ames. If you're not Macklin, who are you?'

'Don't let's get involved in a quiz session, chum. I am Macklin. Eve sent me to talk with you. Eve's a woman.'

'So what? Is there something special about her? Believe me, if there is I didn't notice.'

Macklin said nothing for a moment. He simply sat there and puffed at his cigarette and considered Ames.

'So you don't think there is anything special about her?' he said at length. 'You were in that prison farm with Mel?'

'Look, I told Eve. Do I have to repeat my story to each one of the rest of you? If so, why don't we all get together and I'll cut a disc that you can play over when you require convincing.'

'Don't get smart with me, chum.' Macklin steadied the gun on Ames' chest. He pretended to take aim, then blew smoke along the barrel. His blue eyes glittered like sparkling beads. 'This game isn't for lollipops.'

Ames straightened his shirtfront and sank down on an easy chair, Macklin's gaze followed his hand to his own cigarettes on the table. Ames brought a cigarette out and lit it. He met the blue eyes squarely.

'Shall I tell you something about yourself?' he said.

A flicker disturbed the concentration in Macklin's gaze, then he nodded.

'Don't make me laugh too much, is all. My sense of humour is somewhat blunted.'

'You're just a noise, Macklin,' Ames said quietly. 'Without the gun you're holding you'd be nothing more than an anonymous speck of dust on that chair. No wonder you let Savage get caught by the cops. No wonder you allowed the dame to pull a sweet trick on you. Eve is special in one way after all. She was able to count the score and realize what it might mean for her. Without Mel there would be a gap in the fraternity. Without Mel there would be a place for the rot to set in. Eve might be a woman, but to me that makes her a woman with a brain.'

'You know all about it,' Macklin sneered. 'Tell me some more, chum.'

'You'd better stop calling me chum,' Ames told him. 'I don't make friends easily; hardly ever with a guy who's prepared to stick a knife in my back. Another thing,' he continued steadily, I'm not so sure I could fit in with your outfit — '

'You haven't been asked,' Macklin interrupted brashly. 'Wait until you are before you get astride your high horse. Eve mentioned a sum Mel promised you. Who's to say what he promised you? He might never get out of prison to be in a position to argue with you.'

'I had a note.'

'I saw the note. I could read what it said. What's the name of the prison farm? Exactly where is it?'

'Sorry, Macklin, that is all wrapped up

in the deal. And don't go having inspirations about roughing me over to make me talk. I'll talk when I'm ready and not before then.'

'When?'

'I'd rather settle that with Eve.'

'The hell with you and Eve, Ames.'

Macklin dropped his cigarette to the floor and rubbed it into powder with his heel. He stood up and put the gun away in his pocket, then he backed off to the door. If he expected Ames to get excited he was mistaken.

'Don't check out of this hotel, chum.'

Still Ames made no response. His stomach ached slightly where the man had taken him off guard. Had he been ready for the blow it would merely have taken the wind out of him.

Macklin opened the door. A faint smile pulled at the corners of his mouth.

'I might drop past again tomorrow,' he murmured.

'I might not be here then,' Ames said. 'I'm easily soured on guys of your calibre.'

'All the same, hang on, mister. A

hundred grand might work wonders for your gripe. And whatever else you do, don't open your mouth. To anybody.'

'You've seen too many gangster movies,' Ames said derisively. 'What you need to get you close to the facts is a spell on a rockpile, Macklin.'

Macklin's smile fled and his mouth turned mean. He started to say something else, changed his mind, and went on out of the room.

* * *

The fat man and then Macklin, Ames thought as he stubbed out his cigarette on a tray and helped himself to another one. They were certainly doing plenty of checking up on him. But he supposed they had learned to be careful. It seemed they each intended to make an appraisal of him before throwing the whole thing open to a vote. That meant he might expect the third male member of the gang soon, to come and look him over.

He had deliberately goaded Macklin in an effort to make his own assessment of the man's potential. Macklin wasn't nearly as dumb as he had told him he was. The man was bright enough, and mean enough to be a very dangerous enemy.

Ames didn't go far from the hotel on the following day either, and he was beginning to have doubts about the setup when noon came and went without any communication from the gang. Later he bought a magazine at the news-stand and sat in the lobby, wondering if the fat man would be his next visitor.

At dark he left the hotel to have a decent meal at the restaurant he had taken a fancy to. He spent an hour over the meal, and on his return to the hotel learned that Mr Mack had been here again.

'He said you were expecting him,' the clerk said with his professional fixed smile. 'I gave him your key. I trust I did the right thing?'

'Of course,' Ames acknowledged and headed for the elevator.

Macklin was standing in the centre of the floor when Ames opened the door of his room and entered. He had his arms folded loosely across his chest and a cigarette was dangling from his lips.

'Where were you?'

'Eating out. I've developed a taste for good food.'

Macklin thought this was funny enough to snigger at.

'Okay,' he said briskly. 'You can start packing your stuff, Ames. You're moving out.'

'To where you guys are holed up?'

'That's right,' Macklin said.

As had been Ames' experience before, the crook was taken completely by surprise when Ames threw a crisp short left to the angle of his jaw. Macklin was sent sprawling on top of the sofa. It was a moment before the glaze left his eyes and he was able to speak.

'What the hell did you do that for?' he spluttered.

'It's a good question, chum,' Ames responded coolly. 'You can mull it over while I'm packing my bag.'

8

Macklin left him and he packed the changes of clothing he had into the suitcase, then he called the desk clerk and told him to have his check ready when he arrived down.

'You're leaving us so soon, Mr Ames? Didn't you find everything to your liking?'

'I'll recommend you on all my travels,' Ames assured him.

He was about to vacate the room when the bellhop turned up. He smiled at Ames and pried into all the corners once more.

'What did you hope to find?'

'A rule of the house, sir. Mr Phipps had a very nasty experience once.'

Ames was willing to go along with that. A man like Phipps was bound to have garnered enough nasty experiences to fill a book.

'Oh,' he said. 'Yes. Mr Phipps is the lad in the lobby. What happened? Did a guest leave a time-bomb behind?'

'Almost as bad. A body.'

Ames pulled an exaggerated grimace. 'Surely not a dead one?'

'It's the way he tells it, sir. I'll carry your suitcase. I'm sorry to see you are leaving.'

'Thanks.' Ames found fifty cents in his pockets. Downstairs, he settled his bill and headed outside to the street. A handsome Oldsmobile was parked at the kerb, the stone-faced Macklin at the wheel.

'You took enough time to have a shave and manicure,' he scowled. 'Where is your heap?'

'On the parking space round back. As for what was holding me up: the manager wasn't sure if he should fumigate the room after you left.'

'I don't like you, Ames.'

'I think you're wonderful,' Ames replied. 'It's a pity we can't get along.'

'It might be a good idea if you left your car someplace,' Macklin said. 'Has it occurred to you that you might have someone following you?'

Ames thought of the fat man, but passed no comment on him.

'That would be a bad idea,' he said to Macklin. 'I've got used to having my own transport. How do I know you're not planning on getting me into your car and then having somebody pop out of the back seat with a cut-throat razor?'

Macklin just stared bleakly at him.

'Suit yourself. Go get your heap and come after me. Don't ride too close, but don't get lost either.' He started the car's engine purring.

Ames walked round to the Dodge and used his keys to open the trunk. He raised the spare wheel and extracted a .38 automatic and shoulder holster. He slipped off his jacket and drew on the harness, pushing the gun into the holster. Then he put the suitcase into the trunk beside his shotgun, slammed the lid, and a moment later was cruising to the street. As soon as Macklin saw him coming he engaged gear and drove off.

* * *

The fat man had been standing in the shadows of a store doorway, sucking at the thick cigar he clenched in his teeth. He had watched all that happened and now he ambled into the hotel lobby and crossed to the desk.

'Yes, sir?' the clerk said, wondering where he had seen the beefy features before. 'Do you want a room?'

'I want to know if Mr Ames is in his room. I'm a friend that he was expecting to call on him.'

'Then you're a little late, sir,' the clerk replied. 'Mr Ames checked out a few minutes ago.'

'Too bad,' the fat man said and smiled meagrely. 'He didn't leave any forwarding address?'

The clerk shook his head.

'He was here for only a few days. It might interest you to know that he had another friend visiting.'

'He always was a popular guy,' the fat man nodded. 'Did you catch the name?'

'Yes, Mack. A Mr Mack.'

'Thanks a lot,' the fat man said and nodded once more.

When he walked to the street the clerk punched at the bell on his desk and the bellhop appeared.

'Did you search that room?'

'Sure, I did, Mr Phipps. I went through it before the gentleman left it.'

'Go up and search again, if you please. Thoroughly this time. I didn't like the look of those people.'

The bellboy shrugged and headed for the elevator. Phipps stared across the lobby at the dark street and frowned for a moment, then he searched for the fifth he kept hidden under a bundle of old files in the bottom drawer.

* * *

Macklin led Ames through a multitude of back streets and alleys before striking out for the centre of town and making his way from there to the northern suburbs. At first his behaviour had given Ames the idea that the gang was holed up in Parkdale, but then he realized that the elaborate detour was designed to frustrate anybody else who might be attempting to follow them.

On a highway at last, Macklin really opened up the Olds, and Ames was forced to tramp hard on the gas pedal to keep the red lights of the receding car in sight. He had the feeling just then that Macklin was deliberately set on irritating him. He had tried to bounce the wind out of Ames and was still gagging on the sample of his own medicine he had received in return.

They had covered fifty miles on the Dodge's speedometer when he saw the car ahead of him commencing to slow. Ames took his cue and slowed too. Macklin's car filtered off the highway on to a side road veering to the left. The crook held his speed down until he had ascertained that Ames was keeping in touch. When the Dodge bobbed on to the side road the Oldsmobile was off once more with the eagerness of a greyhound leaving a trap.

An hour later they were threading through the streets of a small town that had an irregular line of high hills hulking in the background. Macklin didn't pause, but went on out of the town. Ames could have a better view of the hills here. It was elevated country and remote enough to make an acceptable hideout.

Five miles out of the town Macklin's Oldsmobile swerved off the main road on to a gravel track that ran under overhanging trees. The car in front was travelling at a crawl, and when Ames glimpsed the lighted window of a house he guessed they had reached the end of their journey.

Macklin parked to the left of a narrow forecourt and Ames drove his own car alongside and looked at the house.

It was a rambling two-storied affair, with a rustic-work front porch. If anyone had asked him to make a snap guess of its age he would have said eighty to a hundred years. Still, it was better than the shack in the woods he had begun to expect.

Macklin alighted first and jerked his head at Ames. The front door was open now and Ames saw the outline of Eve Birchall's figure. She was wearing slacks and a sweater and her hair hung loosely about her shoulders in a dark mass.

'Did you bring him?' she said to Macklin.

'Well, he's here, isn't he? What the hell, Ames. Are you rooted to that seat?'

His mode of addressing Eve gave Ames a hint of the relationship existing between them. Macklin sounded curt and edgy, as though he had been patient for a long time, but his patience was gradually running out. It added a touch to the picture painted by Mel Savage. The woman had grasped the whip handle at the beginning, but had been hard put to hold on to it ever since.

Ames got out of his car and approached the steps leading to the porch. Eve Birchall's eyes glowed darkly on him.

'Hello again,' she said in an emotionless voice.

'Hello yourself,' Ames grunted.

'Okay, okay,' Macklin growled. 'Now that you've sniffed around each other, let's get inside. I'm dying for a drink.'

Eve preceded Ames along a narrow hall. Inside, there was a fusty, defeated odour about the house. A staircase led off the hall, as did three or four doors on the right. Eve opened the first door she came to and Ames followed her. It was a large living room, with ancient, sober furniture that toned in with the general atmosphere. There was a man loafing on an easy chair by the fire in the hearth.

'Hi,' he said to Ames and rose to his feet.

'Hi,' Ames said.

The man was in his late twenties, a lean, swarthy-skinned type, with a gaunt face and closely-cropped fair hair. He was clad in uncreased slacks and a heavy wool sweater. He reminded Ames vaguely of some of the paintings he had seen of eighteenth-century poets. Had he allowed his hair to grow longer he might have cashed in on his dissipated good looks. His eyes were his weakest point. They were a shade too small and too closely set in his narrow forehead. Also, they were a shade too shifty to invite much trust.

'This is Dave Huggins,' Eve said when her gaze had shuttled between the two men for a moment. 'Are you hungry?' she added in the same emotionless voice.

Ames shook his head. Huggins had detected the slight bulge under Ames left armpit. He stepped forward and jerked his coat back, grinning crookedly as he did so.

'Loaded for bear, huh?'

'Call it being cautious.'

'Well, you don't have to be that cautious with us, pal. You're amongst friends.'

'Time will tell,' Ames said.

The shifty eyes switched from Ames to Eve.

'You weren't far wrong, honey,' he said. 'This guy could be a lot of trouble if he isn't handled properly.'

'You want to try handling me?' Ames murmured.

Macklin cleared his throat roughly.

'This is all we need now,' he lamented. 'A lighted match tossed in on the dry straw. Look, Ames, take it easy, will you. Take the weight off your feet and I'll get you a drink.'

'A good idea,' Huggins agreed. He went back to his chair by the hearth and sank into it. He brought cigarettes from the table at his hand and placed one between his lips. All the while his gaze remained on Ames, absorbing him, testing him, wanting to arrive at some definite conclusion.

Ames sat down on a sofa and Eve took the chair opposite him. The pale face was a mask that effectively shielded her private thoughts. She had taken a lot from these men, he saw. But she had not given an inch in her determination to have her way.

Macklin went to a makeshift bar in a corner of the room where a lot of empty bottles and dirty glasses were stacked. He reached under the bar for a full bottle and hunted in the cupboard for more glasses.

'How do you like your scotch, Ames? I hope you like it straight, or with water. It's all there is,' he appended with a faint sneering twist to his mouth.

'So long as it's whisky, I'm ready for it.'

'How about you, Eve?'

'Nothing,' the woman said. She was lighting a cigarette and Ames noticed that her fingers shook ever so slightly. So she wasn't as calm and controlled as she wanted everybody to believe, he thought. He was convinced she was definitely apprehensive.

'Never mind,' Macklin said. 'One of us at least should keep his wits about him.'

He brought Ames his drink first. It was a tall glass and was generously filled, with very little water. He served the swarthy Huggins next, then he walked to the fireplace with his own drink, leaning an elbow on the mantlepiece. Ames was the centre of their concerted attention.

'Okay, Lew,' Macklin urged after a moment of silence had gone by. 'Let's have it. We're gathered like one big happy family, and now we're ready to listen to what you've got to say.'

Ames had sensed there was something missing, and it struck him what it was.

'Mel gave me to understand there were four members of the team. So far I've seen only the three of you. Is Milo Farland so bashful?'

'He isn't here,' Eve answered slowly. Her gaze clashed with Ames' and locked briefly.

'What happened to him?' He was

thinking of the fat man again. So the fat man just had to be Milo Farland. They had planned his reception this way, leaving Farland out of it so that he might view the overall picture from a different vantage point.

'He went away,' Art Macklin explained carelessly. 'I don't blame him,' he added with a touch of bitterness directed at the woman. 'We've sat around on our rumps until we've practically taken root. Milo was the exception. He found he didn't root that easy.'

'You mean he parted company?'

'I told you,' Macklin said with a trace of impatience. 'Going away and parting company are the one thing.'

'When did this happen?' Ames pressed.

'Oh, hell,' Macklin exploded. 'I don't know. I'm not sure. Six months maybe. A year. We're living in a world where time stands still.'

Ames said nothing for a short space. If they were intent on bluffing him he ought to tell them it wasn't working.

'What does Farland look like?' he said over the rim of his glass.

'Rock me gently! What do you figure he looks like? He's got two legs and a head — '

'Is he fat or thin?'

Macklin threw his hands in the air in a gesture of hopelessness. If he missed the point that Ames was concentrating on, Eve didn't. Something approaching animation caught at her fragile features.

'What are you really driving at?' she asked Ames.

'He's putting off the evil hour,' Macklin snorted. 'I tell you, he's as suspicious as be damned. I'm beginning to get a hunch about him too.'

Eve started to speak but Ames waved her roughly to silence. Huggins seemed to have swallowed a mouthful of whisky the wrong way and began to cough.

'Let's have this hunch you're talking about,' Ames urged.

'Well, how do we know? You could be pulling a stall. What proof do we have that you ever saw Mel? That you were ever in any prison? You said you worked on a farm, didn't you? Let's have a gander at your hands.'

'You felt the weight of one of them. I hardly touched you, but you bent under it like you'd been hit by an atom bomb.'

'This guy is funny,' Dave Huggins said. 'This guy is the best entertainment we've had in years. And, boy, do we need comedy about the house! Did he sock you, Art?'

'He socked me and I socked him back,' Ames explained tersely.

'That right, Art?'

'Yeah,' Macklin admitted.

'Why?' Eve asked Macklin.

'I don't know. It just happened. Look, we're getting away from the main theme.'

'You saw the note he brought,' Eve said to Macklin. 'It was plain enough. I recognized Mel's handwriting, even if you didn't.'

'I'm not trying to bust the deal, Eve. But I just want to be sure.'

'Let him see your hands,' Eve ordered Ames.

He spread them and Huggins got out of his chair to look.

'Put them back where they came from, pal,' he winced. 'They remind me of hard work.'

'What do you think?' Ames said to Macklin.

'I've still to be convinced,' was the measured response. 'By the time you get the whole story off your chest we might have progressed to a better understanding.'

Ames swallowed the dregs of his glass.

'Mel promised me a hundred grand to contact you,' he said.

'He must have lost a few marbles,' Huggins remarked. 'A hundred grand would tear the loot practically down the middle.'

'Who planned the job?'

'That doesn't come into it,' Macklin argued. 'It was a team effort. One of us couldn't have done it without the other.'

'Mel planned it,' Eve said crisply. 'He was the brains of the outfit and it gives him the right to decide how it should be carved up.'

'Don't start that all over again,' Macklin scowled at her. 'We're all aware of the torch you're carrying for Mel. If you'd been sensible and played square with us, we wouldn't be sitting here now.

I wouldn't, for sure. If the dough is going to be split, Mel will be here when the splitting's done. You've sung that tune in our ears often enough. Okay, let it ride. You want us to spring him, and this guy's supposed to have the blueprint for doing it. It's time he told us what it is.'

'Just a minute,' Eve said, her gaze on Ames. 'Why are you so curious to hear what Milo Farland looks like?'

Ames wondered if he should pursue the subject. But why not? If these three harboured the idea that Milo Farland had decided to relinquish his share of the bank haul, and all the while Farland was hanging around, like a buzzard awaiting the right moment to descend on the pickings, it could very well lead to dangerous complications later on. Better to let them know so that provision could be made to cope with him, than to risk being caught in the middle of a backlash at the wrong moment.

'Because I believe I've seen Farland in Parkdale,' he told the woman.

A tense silence followed his statement.

Macklin broke it with a harsh derisive laugh.

'See what I mean,' he jeered. 'I wouldn't trust this guy out of my sight. You might as well — '

'Shut up, Art,' Eve commanded sharply. Her eyes were narrow pinpoints on Ames' face. 'This man you take to be Milo, Ames. Tell me what he looked like.'

'He looked fat. He smokes large cigars.'

'That wasn't Milo Farland,' Eve said tautly. 'Milo is not fat, nor does he smoke any sort of cigar. Don't you see,' she went on scathingly. 'Somebody has been following you all the way.'

9

Ames remembered a time, some years ago, when he had been courting a girl called Wendy Grady. He had thought he was quite a big-shot then, rather sharp and witty, and no end of a charmer. They had been necking in the moonlight on the Grady's back porch when this man had rumbled out of the darkness, taking a few shaky steps forward, a few backward. He fell flat on the ground and commenced singing drunkenly.

'Do you know,' Ames had muttered in the ear of the girl. 'If I thought I would ever let myself be taken over like that, I'd bind myself to a railroad tie and take the clean and fast way out.'

He had expected the girl to have a giggle over this, at the very least; instead she had frozen momentarily, staring at the man lying on the ground.

'That happens to be my father,' she said. She had gone forward to help her father and Ames had proceeded to do likewise. The girl, however, had different ideas. 'Goodnight, Mr Ames,' she had said coldly. 'Don't bother to call for me tomorrow evening.'

Ames had been fresh out of college, with the notion that he was sufficiently equipped to stride blithely over every obstacle that had the temerity to rise up before him. The girl's snub had taken the wind from him, left him with a weak, numbed feeling in the pit of his stomach. He had not believed that this could happen to him, but it had. There was a lesson in it that it would pay him to observe. Think twice at least before you speak.

He had thought twice at least over the advisability of mentioning the fat man. He had thought more than twice about it. Even so, he knew he had committed a blunder.

There could be two sides to it, of course. If he was to accept what the woman was telling him, then the fat man was not Milo Farland, but somebody else. If he was to suspect what Eve was telling him, it could mean that they had given Milo Farland the task of watching him from afar and now they were ready to deny it.

'Maybe he has put on weight since you last saw him,' he said to Eve. 'Maybe too, he has developed a taste for large cigars.'

'Never mind what he has or hasn't done,' the woman snapped bitterly. 'Was he following you around?'

'He could have been.'

'He could have been,' Macklin parroted. 'Dames! Just leave everything to me, she says. I know that one day Mel will get in touch with the old hideout, she says. If he can't do it himself, he'll find somebody to do it for him — '

'Shut up,' Eve stormed at him. 'How was I to know Mel would use some guy that doesn't have a brain in his head?'

'Oh, Ames has brains all right,' Macklin scowled. 'And don't you forget that he has. He weighed this up. He saw what could be in it for him. What he doesn't know is that he's just another sword sent by courtesy of Mel Savage to dangle over us.'

'One thing at a time,' Huggins interposed. 'How often did you spot this fat man?'

'Twice,' Ames responded.

'What were the circumstances?'

Ames described his noticing the stranger in the lobby of the hotel in Parkdale, and how he had seen him again as he had been leaving the movie theatre.

'I think I've got the picture,' Huggins said. 'You're sure you never saw this man before or since?'

'Are you sure he isn't Milo Farland?' Ames countered.

'He isn't Milo. You'd never mistake Milo for fat in a hundred years. Also, he smokes a pipe. He can't stand cigarettes or cigars. So rid yourself of the idea that this character was Milo Farland. Now, you say you saw him a couple of times. The first time in the lobby of the hotel in Cooper Street. Next you saw him when you left the movie theatre. You saw him in the light, and you saw him in the dark. Right?'

'What are you building up to?' Macklin said to Huggins. 'If he says he saw this fat man twice, then he must have seen him twice.'

'Or imagined he did,' Huggins insisted.

'Why should he imagine things?'

'Maybe if you'd had a spell at that prison farm, it might have done things to your imagination as well,' Ames told him. Dave Huggins was unwittingly casting a rope to him that he meant to grab and hold on to grimly. It had flashed to Ames' mind who the fat man could really be — an agent assigned by Edward Ogden to keep a fatherly eye on him. It didn't exactly fit in with what Ames had come to accept as the pattern of the chief's conduct, but perhaps Ogden had wondered if a man who had been out of active circulation for a year would not have accumulated a little hampering rust. The chief had the right to act contrary to his wishes if he deemed it necessary. Therefore, if the fat man was a paternal figure in the scheme of things, the truth must be shielded from this gang at all costs.

'You and your prison farm!' Macklin rounded on Ames. He strode across to stand in front of Ames. 'Did you see this guy more than once, or didn't you?'

'Now you've got me confused — '

'Like hell you're confused. You look in the pink of health. You might be too damn healthy to stay around here for long.'

The implication was not lost on Ames, nor did Eve Birchall miss the intended barb. Before Ames could speak she moved swiftly forward and brought her hand whipping against Macklin's jaw.

The man swore and went to grab her. Ames and Dave Huggins acted in concert, each of them catching one of Macklin's arms and pinning them to his sides.

Macklin struggled pantingly, obscenities spewing from his lips. He appeared to exercise a vast effort at self-control and finally subsided.

'Take your hands off me,' he growled at the two men.

They released him and he stood, chest heaving, eyes fixed balefully on the woman.

'You prod and you prod,' he breathed. 'But one of these times you're going to prod me too far, Eve. When that happens, look out. I'm telling you.'

If he thought to browbeat Eve he was mistaken. She returned his hot glare with a chill regard.

'Very well,' she said at length. 'I'll lay off prodding if you lay off your dirty insinuations. And listen to me, all three of you,' she continued vibrantly. 'If you don't settle down and be sensible, the deal is off. Even with Ames coming in with his chips. You'll get out of bed some morning and I'll have flown the coop. You can search till hell freezes over, but you won't find me. Nor will you find the money. Is that clear?'

A retort boiled to Macklin's tongue, but he bit it down. He slouched over to the bar and set about pouring himself another drink. He took a stool there and drank silently. Huggins exchanged glances with Ames. There was a lot more to Huggins than Ames had guessed. If there was a strong hand amongst the trio it belonged to Huggins, and not Eve, as he had deduced earlier.

He shrugged and went back to his chair.

'You people have been living on top of each other for far too long,' he remarked calmly. 'You've reduced yourselves from responsible adults to the level of moronic kids.'

'Forgive me if I don't applaud your sparkling wisdom,' Eve returned drily. 'You don't know the first thing about it. The point is, we have stuck together. As Dave has said, you could have been nervous enough in Parkdale to imagine a fat man was interested in you. We'll keep our eyes peeled for a fat man. And now, what about telling us what Mel arranged with you?'

'I'm bushed,' Ames said. 'My mind is going round in circles. How would it do if we let the whole thing ride until the morning?'

'And give you time to figure out a different story?' Macklin grunted from the bar. 'Like I said, Ames, I don't trust you the way Eve's prepared to trust you. And this fat guy. He might be a figment of your imagination or he might not. But

I'm not dumb. You were a pal of Mel's at that prison farm. The authorities know why Mel is there. The feds know why he's there. They know Mel was part of the outfit that took a quarter of a million bucks from a bank in Maytown. The rest of the outfit were never caught. The quarter million bucks was never found.'

'You're saying that the authorities might have put a tail on me?' Ames queried, at the same time simulating wonder.

'I'm saying they might. They could work it out that Mel and you were hatching up a plot.'

'They could work it out also that the dough is still on ice? That the outfit is still sitting with its fingers crossed hoping for a miracle to turn Mel loose?'

'I go for your angle,' Huggins said to Ames. 'Who's going to stick around for years in the hope of all the pieces clicking together?'

'The feds might,' Macklin maintained. He glanced at Eve for confirmation of his theory, but the woman was studying the lighted tip of a cigarette.

'Let him get on with it,' she said patiently. 'The sooner Mel's a free man again, the sooner I can have you moaners off my back. All right, Ames,' she added. 'The bargain is this: if what you have to say helps us to release Mel from the prison farm, then it rests between you and Mel how much he pays you for your help.'

'He offered me a hundred grand. If we do manage to spring him I'll see he keeps his word.'

'You do that, buster,' Macklin sneered.

* * *

He gave them the plot precisely as Mel Savage had put it to him. Macklin listened for a few minutes as though he wasn't much interested one way or the other, but it wasn't long before he was sitting on the edge of the chair beside the big stranger, swallowing every word he had to say.

Ames smoked cigarettes while he talked. Talking brought back the prison farm with a vividness that surprised him.

He had believed himself to have thrown off the experiences he had been through like a discarded jacket. It wasn't so. The prison farm had been as real and as tormenting to him as it had been to any of the other inmates. He had felt the bite of Burt Lashley's tongue, the punishing weight of the sadist's fists. He recalled the long, lonely nights, nights when he had needed to bring every atom of his patience and selfconfidence to bear. Whilst at the farm he had been a prisoner, and as he had expressed to Edward Ogden, he had thought like a prisoner. As he had seen it at the outset, it was the only reliable method of breaking the gang and finding out what had become of the quarter million dollars they had stolen.

He was tense and strung-up by the time he had finished. During the recital Eve Birchall had stood before him, her dark eyes never leaving his features. Now in the heavy silence all three of them regarded him with a deep concentration.

Dave Huggins emitted a soft whistle.

'You know what you've just done man?'

he said throatily. 'You've laid a lump of ice a yard wide along my spine.'

Macklin had no comment to make on his own reactions. He went over to the bar and came back with the whisky bottle.

'Say when,' he told Ames.

'I've drunk enough.'

'You only think you have, chum. Go on, knock it back.'

Obediently Ames helped himself to the fresh drink. He raised his eyes then to Eve.

'It sounds simple enough. The farm is near Blandon, like I said. There's nothing but open country all around. From the road you should be able to see the prisoners with a set of highpowered binoculars. You might even see Mel.'

She drew a sharp breath at that, jerking out of her own thoughts. Her breast heaved under the stress of some emotion. Instead of replying to Ames she turned to Macklin.

'How far from here to Blandon?'

'I'll get out the map,' Macklin said. He started over the floor to leave the room.

'I reckon it to be in the region of five hundred miles,' Ames told them.

At the door Macklin wheeled to stare at him.

'How did you make it from there to Delton City?'

'By bumming rides. In trucks and cars. It wasn't so easy.'

'I'll go get the map,' Macklin said. 'We'll have to work out the best route.'

'Then you're going to go through with it?'

'Hell yes. What do you figure we're going to do — sit here for another year and talk about it? But, Ames, it all better be on the level.'

'Aw, knock it off, Art.' This from Huggins. 'The guy told you everything, didn't he? He says Mel made a pal of him and I believe him.'

'There's another good point,' Macklin murmured. 'You and Mel becoming so friendly. Howcome?'

'Mel didn't pick on me because of my handsome looks,' Ames replied. 'He was like you, Art. Like Dave there. Like Eve there. He had his angle. If I'd been a long-term prisoner he wouldn't have given me a second thought. He knew I was going out in a year. I was a straw to grab at and he grabbed me with both hands. I'll tell you something else now that I'm warmed up,' Ames continued. 'He asked me to make for your old hideaway and to stay there for a month. If nothing clicked as he fancied it might, he put another proposition to me.'

'Yeah? Well, don't clam up when you're going so good, chum. What was the other proposition?'

'He asked me to do a solo act with a car. I would go through with the original plan, and if he made it to safety we'd go after the bank loot together. If and when we found it he would split straight down the middle with me.'

'The crafty sonofabitch!'

'I call it fighting for survival.'

'He knew he could trust me,' Eve said weakly.

'He sure talked about you as though you were an extraordinary woman, Eve. He depended on you all right. He's still depending on you.'

'I won't let him down,' she said more steadily. 'Even — even if Art and Dave back out at this stage, we'll do it together, Ames.'

'Hey, hey! Let's drop this duet pitch. If you think Dave and I are back-tracking now, you're nuts.'

'I was merely saying — '

'Okay, okay, I heard you, Eve. You and Mr Good Looking are going no place and doing nothing without us sitting in the back seat to cheer you on.'

'It's decided then?' Slow colour was creeping into her pale cheeks. 'We do it, and we do it soon?'

'We do it and we do it soon, baby.'

Macklin went on out to get the map. Eve walked over to the window and lifted the blind slightly to peer out at the dark night.

'It might work and it might not,' Huggins declared suddenly. 'I mean, you shouldn't build yourself up to any great steam, Eve.'

'I'm not building myself up to anything,' she retorted heatedly. 'There is only one problem that I can visualise. You say the guards are hard and that they think nothing of turning the dogs on an escaping prisoner.'

'Mel is convinced he can make it,' Ames replied reassuringly. 'He's been there long enough to know if he can.'

She left the window and came across to stand before him once more. Ames read a blossoming of hope in her eyes, but there was a counteracting measure of anxiety.

'What do you think?' she asked Ames. 'Tell me truly what your own opinion of his chances are.'

'I think he's got a good chance. The fact that I'm here at all should be enough proof for you.'

'He would have to get clear of the fields. Then he would have to get clear of the woods you spoke of. Supposing the dogs were turned loose before he managed to reach the woods?'

'That wouldn't be so good.'

'Then none of it is good,' she cried in a burst of frustration. 'I don't want to see him caught by a pack of hungry dogs, like — like a wild animal.'

'And you don't want him to remain in prison?'

'Yes, yes! I'd rather he remained in prison than that he tried to escape and was torn to pieces.'

'Then you don't know Mel Savage as well as you believe you do, Eve. I was close to him for a whole year. I heard his gripes, his dreams. I can make a reasonable assessment of his own sentiments on the matter. If I'd had to stay there for just one more year I'm sure I'd have gone crazy. Either you go crazy or you allow yourself to be turned into an automaton.'

'But Mel isn't crazy?'

'Slow down, Eve, will you. Of course he isn't crazy. If he is, then I'm in the same boat. I listened to him. I paid heed to him. I took him for a sane person. I wouldn't be talking to you now if I'd thought otherwise.

'There is another slant on this that I'd better mention. They talk at the camp of how prisoners have tried to escape and of how they were caught. I won't go into any gory details. But the head warden plays a game with his escapers — '

'A game?'

'I guess it's what he calls it. Anyhow, if a man does make an escape bid, it's popularly believed that the head warden lets him get far enough away from the compound to kid himself he's really going to make it, before he turns in the alarm. It's this that Mel is banking on. He's sure he can run and keep running until he reaches the country road. Normally it would be the point where the prisoner's luck ran out.'

'But not if there was a car waiting?' Dave Huggins interposed. 'I get you now, Ames.'

'He could still be caught,' Eve panted. 'I would never forgive myself if he was caught.'

'There's only one way of putting it to the test,' Ames told her. 'You take the risk or you don't.'

At that moment Art Macklin returned with the large-scale map he had gone to look for.

10

Ames awoke with a start and jerked up on his elbow, the better to listen to whatever it was had disturbed him. The bed creaked. Everything seemed to creak in the small bedroom that had been allotted him. The floorboards had creaked earlier underfoot. The door creaked as though its hinges had never been oiled since the day of fitting. So did the single chair that leaned drunkenly against the dresser. Ames had made the mistake of sitting on it to take off his shoes. It had threatened to collapse beneath his weight.

There was a hard wind against the house. It sang through the surrounding trees and shrubbery and mourned in the eaves. Possibly too it was working at a loose shutter on a downstairs window, and that had provided the noise to bring him awake.

He heard it again and peered into the shadows at the room door. Someone had just tapped lightly on the panelling. It must have been an earlier rapping that had awakened him.

Flinging the bedclothes aside, Ames stretched his hand to the .38 snugged in its shoulder harness that was draped over the bedpost. He didn't like the people in this house any more than he liked the house itself. There was an atmosphere faintly reminiscent of the prison farm. The same kind of emotions existed here — resentment, yearning for freedom, even if on a different level, ugly tempers that were constantly simmering and which would require the tiniest spark to cause an eruption. This house was a prison for the three people living in it, and their temperaments had clashed so often they each knew the other like a well-read book that had become unbearably boring.

With his gun at the ready Ames tip-toed to the door, favouring the boards he knew had the greatest capacity for creaking. He slid the latch and drew the door open.

Eve Birchall, a bathrobe wrapped

around her, stood in the opening. She took a step backwards at sight of the .38 and Ames lowered it to his side.

'What's the matter?' he whispered. 'Can't you get to sleep?'

'I want to talk with you.'

He caught her arm and drew her on into the room, aware of a tingling of excitement teasing his nerves. He closed the door gently behind him. He sensed her recoiling instinctively from his touch and released his fingers.

'Okay. You don't have to be frightened of me. I'm too tired to get amorous, even if you wanted me to.'

'I don't want you to,' she said flintily. 'And before we go any further, get one thing into your head. I'm no easy mark. No matter what Art hinted at, I'm not.'

Ames made a display of stifling an elaborate yawn. The excitement had passed out of his system and now he was merely curious concerning the reason for her visit.

'Then why leave yourself open to the gossips? Incidentally, Mel would be mighty proud of you.'

He heard the soft hissing of her breath in the shadows.

'I said I wanted to talk with you. Alone. Where neither of them can hear us.'

'They stick close to you, I guess?'

'They never let me out of their sight. It's — it's like being in chains for twenty-four hours of every day. The only privacy I get is in the bathroom. At that, I dare say they take turns at peeping through the keyhole.'

'You must be having a real keen time.'

'Are you going to snigger about it?' Her voice was bitter.

'Slow down, Eve. Who's sniggering? Have a seat on the edge of the bed. I'll switch on the lamp.'

'No,' she said quickly. 'Leave the lamp alone. We can talk just as well in the darkness.'

'Please yourself by all means. Cigarette?'

She shook her head, continuing to stand before him despite his invitation to sit down. A wave of subtle fragrance drifted to his nostrils. His eyes were growing accustomed to the gloom and now he could discern the pale outline of her features, the brushed out mass of her hair. Her own eyes glistened on him. He tried guessing at the thoughts running in her brain. A hunch had occurred to him, but it must stay in abeyance until the woman explained.

'I want you to help me, Ames.'

She paused there, waiting for him to respond, but he said nothing. He groped for his cigarettes on the table and placed one between his lips. He had to grope again before he found his lighter. He lit the cigarette and puffed a cloud of smoke into the air.

'Did you hear what I said?'

There was a sharp edge to her voice, a faint note of desperation. She moved closer to him and laid her hand on his arm.

'I hear you, Eve.'

'Then why the hell can't you say something? Why do you stand there like a big stupid dummy?'

'You'd better keep your voice down,' he warned. 'Else you'll have your two playmates beating on the walls for us to keep quiet so they can sleep.'

'Would you be willing to help me?'

'That's better,' Ames murmured. 'That's a whole lot better, Eve. I've grown tired of taking orders. It's a pleasant change to hear somebody making a request. But you should have said please.'

'You're laughing up your sleeve at me. Okay, go ahead and laugh your silly head off. But I thought you might be smart enough to heed a word of warning.'

'Warning? Warning against what? Your boyfriends?'

'They're not my boyfriends,' she said with passion. 'They're just two leeches that intend to hang on until the last breath. Do you really trust them? Do you think they trust you?'

'I don't trust anybody,' Ames replied coolly. 'Therefore I don't expect a lot of trust to be put in me.'

'You talk like a seasoned criminal,' she jeered. 'What did you ever rate outside of running over a man in a car?'

'Let it ride,' Ames said. He dropped his cigarette into a bowl and sat down on the edge of the bed. 'Come and be comfortable, Eve.'

'You cheap louse!'

'Have it your way if you must. Me, if people expect me to be nice with them, then they sure as satan have to learn to be nice with me.'

'A right friend of Mel's you've turned out to be,' she said scornfully. Yet he sensed a weakening of her attitude. She was a woman who had closed herself off from everything and settled down to concentrate on a bright light that shone clearly ahead of her. Ames fancied the light was commencing to dim, or it might have dimmed already and she was still holding on, in the hope that it would come to life again.

A silence came between them and ran on for the space of thirty seconds. Then Eve crossed to the bed and sat down beside him. Ames drapped an arm around her shoulders, at the same time feeling her tighten up and go tense.

'Relax.'

'Easier said than done.'

She laughed softly, but it wasn't really a laugh. He drew her closer to him and found her lips with his mouth. It was like kissing a lump of ice and he didn't keep it going.

'What are you waiting for?' she said hoarsely. 'For me to catch fire?'

'You don't burn easy, baby. That guy stinking in the prison farm must be a very proud man.'

She jerked away from him and her breathing came shallowly and rapidly. Her eyes were twin, dancing flares.

'Leave Mel out of it. But you take me and you're bound. If you try a double-cross, ever, I'll find some way of killing you.'

'Then it's nothing but a straight sale? No give and take.'

'You want to have everything, don't you?' she said curtly.

Ames lay back on the bed and considered her rigid shoulders. 'You've just brought me up short,' he said. 'That gag about being bound, I mean. Perhaps I'd better listen to the entire story before I take what you're not offering.'

She sprang to her feet and he thought she was going to leave the room. She did take a couple of steps across the floor, but halted and looked round at him.

'Can you forget I ever came here, Ames?'

'You've spoiled a night's sleep for me, Eve. But if you mean will I tell Dave and Art about the marvellous chance I passed up, then the answer is that I won't.'

She went on to the door. Ames spoke after her.

'Wait.'

'Wait for what?'

'I'm getting curiouser and curiouser. I don't think you should leave me until you put me out of my suspense.'

'What's the use?' she said wearily. 'I thought you were a little different from them. Well, you look slightly different and you behave slightly different — '

'I get it. Neither Art nor Dave would have turned their nose up at the chance of rumpling you in the feathers, willingly or unwillingly.'

'That's another cheap crack, Ames.'

'I know. I can't help them bubbling out of me. But you did get me awake and you might as well get it off your chest. Excuse me, your bosom.'

Ames was coming off the creaky bed when a sound, that had nothing to do with bed or the wind blowing, made him freeze. Eve had heard it too and uttered a little groan.

'There's somebody in the passage!'

She had scarcely spoken the words when there was a brisk tapping at the bedroom door.

'Are you awake, Ames?' Art Macklin's voice, thick and suspicious.

Ames realized it could be the second stage of a trick. The initial stage had gone into operation with Eve Birchall tapping on the door. They wanted to trap him in a compromising situation, for some reason that he didn't understand yet.

The sharp digging of the woman's fingers into the flesh of his arm told him he was wrong.

'I've got to hide.'

'Take it easy. The latch is on. How about the closet?'

She knew roughly where it was and Ames helped her find it. The closet was little bigger than a phone booth, but Eve squeezed into it and Ames closed the door.

'Do you hear me, mister?' Macklin said.

'Coming.'

He threw the latch, not thinking to switch on the lamp. Macklin strode into the room and did it for him.

'What's going on here?' he growled while his cold blue eyes travelled the length and breadth of the room.

Ames yawned and stretched his arms above his head. He was wearing nothing but pyjamas. He met the sharp gaze that swivelled to pin him.

'I heard somebody talking.'

'Yeah, you did,' Ames scowled. 'You heard me talking in my sleep. What's with all the jumpy, nervous stuff?'

Macklin ignored the gibe, peering over the room once more. His attention centred on the closet door.

'You smoke in your sleep as well?' He sniffed; a frown pulled at his square-jawed features.

'So there is a rule against smoking in bed? A rule against talking in your sleep?

If you want to hear the facts, chum, I wasn't talking in my sleep.'

'But I heard talking.'

'Why pick on me? Try friend Dave. Try Eve. I wouldn't be surprised if the dame was talking to herself. A couple of years with you guys and anybody would go nuts.'

'Is that so?' Macklin sneered. 'Well, Eve doesn't happen to be in her room at all.'

Ames adopted an ugly grimace.

'What a prize punk you are, Art. You mean to tell me she has to ask permission to go to the bathroom.'

'She isn't in the bathroom. I've looked.'

'Maybe she's skipped,' Ames suggested. 'And don't say she didn't warn us what she might do.'

The possibility hadn't really occurred to Macklin, but now it did. With a curse he swung to the door and tramped off along the passage. Ames looked out to see him making for the landing. He began to descend. Ames scrambled over to the closet and pulled the door open. Eve's eyes were beacons of fright in her pale face.

'Make it back to your room snappy, honey. He could have roused Dave as well.'

'See if the passage is clear. My room is right at the end of it. Dave's is across the way.'

Ames looked out again. Macklin had switched on the faint bulb that glowed in the centre of the ceiling. He stepped into the passage to make sure Huggins' door was closed. It was and he gestured to Eve.

'What excuse will I give him?'

Ames could think of nothing on the spur of the moment. Then he had an inspiration.

'Come to the head of the stairs. If I signal to come down, come down. When you do, make a dash for the kitchen. Say you were thirsty and wanted a drink of water.'

'But Art — '

'I believe he's gone outside to check if the cars are there.'

So saying, Ames dashed on to the landing and went down the stairs two at a time. The front door was open, which proved that Macklin actually had left the house to investigate. Ames went to the front and heard feet scrunching on the gravel. He waved his hand to Eve at the top of the stairs.

She came down them so fast she stumbled on the last step but one and would have fallen had Ames not grabbed her and steadied her. He thrust her on into the hall.

'Beat it, quick.'

He hurried outside then, meeting Macklin on his way in. He startled Macklin for a moment.

'What the hell are you playing at?' the crook growled sourly.

'Did you see her?' Ames countered.

'No, I didn't see her. I — ' He stopped speaking to stare over Ames' shoulder. Ames turned to look at Eve coming from the far wing of the house. She contrived to appear surprised at finding them there.

'What in heaven's name is the matter with you two?' she demanded in her flat, impersonal voice.

'Where the devil were you?' Macklin flashed back at her.

'I came down to get a drink of water.

I — ' She faked dawning comprehension. 'Oh, now I get it. You thought I had taken off someplace. Well, maybe I will one of these nights. But if I do, I'll be a long way away before you ever realize it.'

'Don't talk that way, Eve.'

'Let her have her dreams,' Ames said.

As he spoke his gaze meshed with Eve's, but only for a second and not long enough for him to analyse what was intended for him to read. A message of congratulation for his fast thinking? A morsel of outright gratitude?

Eve went past them and began climbing the stairs. She had marvellously turned calves and ankles. Halfway up she halted and swung to look down at them.

'Take a heavy tip from me,' she said. 'Both of you. Let me have a little privacy when I need it, huh?'

'Your wish is my command, fair one,' Ames said blithely.

Macklin only scowled and said nothing. Eve reached the landing and went from sight. Then Macklin went back to the door and slammed it vigorously.

'I don't trust her,' he said.

'But then you wouldn't be running true to your character if you did, Art.'

'Don't give me any of this hanky-panky stuff, Ames. I'm not blind. I'm not stupid.'

'So?' Ames urged.

'She wasn't down here when I came down first of all. I'm sure of it.'

'This I don't like. Are you hinting she might have been studying witchcraft on the side?'

'I'm saying we'll have to watch her. You especially, pal.'

'Howcome I'm so special?'

'She figures you might not be all that you say you are.'

Ames frowned slightly. If Macklin was planning to throw him he couldn't be any more obvious about it.

'I'm not a man for bragging. I'm modest enough. And right now too I'm as sleepy as sin.'

He started for the stairs.

'Hold it, Ames.'

'Don't let's stir up a mare's nest, Art. Why don't you head back to the feathers yourself. You'll see things differently in the morning.'

'You're not taking this too seriously, are you?'

Ames shrugged, his frown returning.

'What's serious? Going around like you had the world on your shoulders? No, sir. Not for this cat.'

'She's planning on dumping us, chum. Not only you and Dave and me, but Mel as well.'

'You've got to be kidding. That or you're plain dumb, fella. She's carrying a torch that's as conspicuous as the Statue of Liberty.'

'Want to take a bet on it?'

Ames was thoughtful for a moment.

'No,' he said slowly. 'I don't. But I'll give you a little information for free, Macklin. I'm in this gag because Mel Savage invited me. I said I would do something for Mel and Mel said he would do something for me.'

'If the dame has her way we'll never get our eyes on the loot again, much less get a share of it to spend.'

'Exactly what are you attempting to put across, Art?'

'I'm levelling with you,' Macklin replied

flatly. 'Nothing more. Just levelling. No matter how she tries to get around you, don't trust her.'

'There's no charge for the advice?'

'Oh, to blazes with you, Ames. Take it or leave it.'

'I'll certainly think about it,' Ames promised.

He went on up the stairs, feeling the weight of the crook's eyes on his shoulders.

11

The next day was Wednesday. It had been Macklin's idea to use the day for working out their plan in detail. On the following day they would leave the house for Blandon. It would take a whole day to make the drive, and, barring accidents, that would put them in Blandon on Friday.

'What happens at the farm on Saturdays?' he had asked Ames.

'Work goes on as usual in the morning. It stops at noon. There might be a film show in the evening, if Colport's in a good mood.'

'You know what I'd like to do with this guy Colport?'

'You and a thousand others, Art. There wouldn't be enough pieces of him to satisfy everybody.'

Saturday was out then, they had decided. If only Ames had come to the house on Monday, they could have made the try for Mel on Friday night.

'You realize who's to blame, don't you?' Ames had said to Macklin. 'I was in Parkdale from late afternoon Friday. I was available on Monday, but you had to play like you were a spy that didn't even know what the cold was.'

'I had to check with Dave and Eve. It was the way we arranged it.'

There was nothing else for it then but to stay in Blandon over the weekend. They would drive out to the road above the prison farm on Monday around noon and give Savage the horn-sounding signal he would understand. Then, on Tuesday at midnight, they would return to the spot and hope that Mel would turn up.

There was a feverishness in Eve Birchall that morning. She cooked breakfast for all of them — giving them fruit juice, eggs and ham. But when they sat down at the table to eat, Eve merely picked at the food. Macklin and Huggins were too busy with their own appetites to pay much heed, but Ames did.

There was more colour in the woman's cheeks than would be usual for her, even allowing for the labour over the hot stove. There was a glitter in her eyes too that hinted of her preoccupation with her private thoughts. She was thinking of Mel Savage, Ames knew. She was closer to him now than she had been in years. The big question dominating all others would be: could they make a success of helping Savage to freedom?

Once she caught him looking at her and her gaze fought with his for an instant before she lowered her head and pretended an interest in her food.

'You certainly haven't lost your touch,' Macklin said by way of compliment presently, thrusting his empty plate aside and thrusting a cigarette between his lips.

'The supplies are about finished,' she answered. 'If we're not moving out until tomorrow, somebody will have to go to the village and buy things.'

'Let me do it,' Ames volunteered. It seemed a golden opportunity to get on the telephone with Edward Ogden and inquire if there was a fat agent on his trail. 'If you make out a list, Evc — '

'Forget it,' Macklin said gruffly. 'I need

cigarettes anyhow. I'll go. At the same time I'll bring back a couple of bottles. If you need any special knick-knacks, Eve, just write them in a note. Most of the storekeepers know me by now. I'm a John B. Wheeler who has rented this dump for my wife and brother-in-law,' he added for Ames' benefit.

'It didn't take much imagination to dream that up,' Ames told him. 'And if the cops wanted to look closer at you, it wouldn't provide any sort of guarantee.'

'Don't knock my imagination, chum,' Macklin responded with a twisted smile. 'I can think up things that might surprise you.'

'I wouldn't doubt it.'

'How about letting me ride into the village with you?' Huggins suggested. 'You could drop me and pick me up in an hour, when I'd circulated a little.'

'You know damn well there isn't a cat-house in the place,' Macklin reminded him.

'Who the blazes mentioned a cat-house?' Huggins rounded on his friend. 'I got to making terms with a little widow down there. She mightn't be exactly merry, but then I never feel like laughing when I'm — '

'Shut up,' Ames burst out fiercely, unable to keep his temper from spilling over. Macklin and Huggins talked as though Eve didn't exist, or they deemed her something less than a woman. It was their method of hitting back at her for her lack of warmth towards them. Ames had never been able to stomach such sly by-play and he didn't think he should swallow this.

'Keep your shirt on,' Eve said with a carelessness real or affected. 'I know the facts of life as well as the next one. That stuff runs off me like a summer shower. You guys are all the same anyhow, so don't try sounding like a preacher. You'd jump me if I let my guard down for a minute — just like these two specimens would.'

Ames stared at her, scarcely able to believe his ears. She was putting on an act, he decided at length. In company such as she found herself in, and in the peculiar situation which existed, her only defence was this brand of aggression.

'Thanks for giving me an insight into myself,' he said curtly and wandered on through the kitchen to the back yard of the house.

He half expected Macklin to come bustling after him, but he didn't. Ames lit a cigarette and wandered to the edge of the yard where thick shrubbery and young fir trees vied for enough space to flourish in. The sky was clearing in the east and a warm sun was sending out fingers of heat through the trailing grey and crimson-tinted clouds. Ames found a smooth boulder and sat down on it.

He was sitting there for five minutes when Macklin emerged. He was wearing an olive windbreaker and his narrow-brimmed hat. A fresh cigarette drooped from the corner of his mouth. Faint humour glowed in his blue eyes as he moved over to Ames.

'Somebody told me you had a thick skin.'

'Lay off, Art.'

Macklin cast a glance at the house and lowered his voice.

'She can see only one thing, chum.

How many times does it have to be spelled out for you?'

'Don't worry, mister. I'm not so blind I can't see where I'm going. I've got Mel's promise.'

'Promise!' Macklin growled scornfully. 'You saw one side of Mel in that prison farm — the side he wanted you to see. Once that dame gets her claws back into him they'll both take a powder and leave us high and dry.'

Ames looked steadily at the other for a few seconds without speaking.

'They can go where they like after I've been paid off,' he said at length. 'But not before.'

A smirk warped Macklin's features.

'Glad you've got that much guts, Lew. Okay. A warning should be enough for anybody. So now we're prepared. So now we'll organize to suit ourselves.'

'How?' Ames wondered. 'You're not really going through with the big effort on Mel's behalf?'

'Of course we're going through with it. But here's what I'm driving at — when it comes to the crunch and we know where the dough's at — we're going to make sure we collect.'

'Doublecross Eve and her lover-boy?' Ames murmured.

Macklin's smile turned ugly.

'I didn't mention a doublecross. But we take our share. Are you in with us?'

'What you're actually trying, Art, is to sell me a proposition. Take sides with you and Dave against Eve and Mel?'

'There you go again,' Macklin complained. 'Turning what I say up the wrong way. What I want to know is, will you make your stand with us if it's necessary?'

'I'm not so sure,' Ames replied thoughtfully. 'I don't go much for running in packs. Even this gag with the three of you in that house is the next best thing to claustrophobia. But I'll mull over all you've told me.'

Macklin sighed.

'We must be thankful for small mercies,' he said. He flung his cigarette away from him. 'Well, I'm off to the village. Anything special you want?'

'You might bring a newspaper.'

Macklin's eyes narrowed.

'I don't get it. What do you need with a newspaper? You're not one of these queers that fancy they're contributing to the national character by keeping in touch with world events?'

'It might pay you to read a paper occasionally, Art. Last one I read told of a gas station holdup near Blakeville. Two men and a dame. The manager of the gas station was in a bad way. He could be dead by now.'

'He isn't dead,' Macklin said. 'He's making a good recovery.'

'Then you do take an interest in events — the local variety at least.'

'Now and then,' Macklin answered in a measured tone. 'You really are a slick fella, Mr Ames.'

'You could say so, Art. But the next gas station you take, play it cooler. I don't want to be associated with a bunch of cheap killers.'

Macklin left him without commenting. He walked round the corner of the house to the front, and a moment later Ames heard a car engine coughing to life.

Ames remained in the sunshine for a

further ten minutes, then he roused when he heard another car engine running. It spun for a minute and went dead. He went round front and saw Dave Huggins with his head under the hood of the dark green Ford that Eve had used to call at Dobbs' farm. Macklin had taken the Oldsmobile, and his own Dodge stood beside the Ford.

Huggins heard his step and glanced out at him. There was a smear of grease on the swarthy man's cheek and he looked slightly peeved about something.

'What's the matter?' Ames asked. 'Sounded like a plug wasn't firing properly.'

'I figured it was only a plug. It's worse. Far as I can see there's a valve sticking.'

'You'll have to lift the head off. Can't you drive it into the village and have it done?'

'I can do it myself,' Huggins explained. 'It's just that I figured I was through with nursing auto engines.'

'Oh. Then you were a mechanic?'

'Yeah, I was.' Huggins grinned briefly. 'I didn't know when I was well off.'

'You could always jack this lark and find another job someplace.'

'Not on your life, Ames. Summer and the good weather is okay for working in a garage. Winters it can be hellish uncomfortable. You could give me a hand to strip these wires while I loosen the cylinder bolts.'

'You just have to be joking,' Ames chuckled. 'Even lifting a spoon these days sets my fingers to tingling. I handled a pickaxe for so goddamn long.'

Ames stood and watched Huggins for several minutes. Then he left him and went round back to enter the house.

Eve was busy in the kitchen, boiling water for the dirty dishes in the sink. She was smoking a cigarette and jerked slightly when she became aware of him.

'You wash and I'll dry,' he said.

Her smile had a faintly bitter edge to it.

'What are you trying to manufacture for yourself, mister — a phoney atmosphere of domestic bliss?'

'It never crossed my mind. But now that you mention it, you'd look pretty cute in a modern kitchen with all those modern gadgets.'

'That'll be the day I won't ever live to see. You can have your modern kitchen units and the nicely smelling guys who want to stir the soup.'

'You're not the domestic type?'

'Look, Ames, let it drift, will you. Times I imagine I've even forgotten what it's like to be a woman.'

'You were near to it last night,' he said and watched the flush of colour that enlivened her pale cheeks.

'Sure I was. I charmed the hell out of you, didn't I? Just like any common or garden zombie.'

'You're out of practice, is all. You've been too long away from a few bright lights and a little soft music. But let me confess about last night. I was bushed, of course. But I really am a guy who doesn't know what it is to buy love.'

'Go hock it, Ames,' she rasped harshly. 'Leave me alone. I wasn't selling myself.'

'I don't think you were. I don't think you could if you tried. Dave is taking the head off your Ford. He'll be busy for an hour or so.'

She gave a derisive laugh.

'And in an hour or so you might drum up enough heat to thaw me out? Don't make me sick, mister.'

'We weren't all born with one-track minds,' Ames said. 'I'm referring to the state you were in last night, and I'm not talking in terms of sex.'

'Let that drift too. In the middle of the night I get bad dreams sometimes. In the mornings they don't seem so bad. I'm getting I can live with almost everything.'

'So you don't want to take me into your confidence?'

'Why should I? Art has beaten me to it. I saw him wagging his tongue with you. He might have been telling you his life-story for the curiosity you showed.'

'What is that intended to mean?'

She scrubbed furiously at a greasy plate. Taking it from the sink it slipped from her hand and Ames managed to catch it before it fell to the floor.

'You ought to keep me around,' he grinned. 'I'm real good at catching things before they fall and break. I've even been known to patch up things that were already broken.'

'Close the door after you when you go out, huh?'

'You're brushing me off?'

'You were never anywhere on me to need brushing off. Just concentrate on earning your hundred grand.'

'That's the point,' Ames said. 'There's a rumour in the air there could be a bust-up that would complicate matters more than somewhat.'

'Art started it?'

'Art doesn't mean to be done out of his share. Neither do I, Eve. He made a strong case against you.'

She finished stacking the wet plates and began to dry them. He detected a reawakening of the feverishness he had noticed in her at breakfast time. She was more worried than she wished him to guess.

'If you must hang around, light a cigarette and give it to me.'

He lit one of his cigarettes and held it for her lips. As they closed over the end of the cylinder their eyes met and fused momentarily.

'So you know what it looks like to me,'

Ames went on. 'I'm an innocent bystander caught in the middle of a nasty accident.'

'You should know about accidents.'

Macklin wants me to be on his and Huggins' side if anything goes wrong. You would like me to be on your side if something did go wrong.'

'Don't start counting your chicks, sonny.'

'You're tougher than I think you are?'

'What did Art say to you?' she countered, betraying the curiosity she had been attempting to hide.

'He gave me a sad story. He has the feeling that you can see nobody but Mel. He has the feeling that you and Mel might take off and leave the rest of us in the lurch.'

'The crummy bastard!'

'The revelation surprises you?'

'It's no revelation to me, friend. He hates my guts. Since we've been together I must have broken six of his teeth. I lost count of the number of hairs I hauled from his head.'

'In defcnce of your honour?'

'Call it what you like. Your wit doesn't

do a thing to me. But I'll put it one way you might understand. If he had that quarter million right now and he offered the whole of it to me for a roll in the hay, do you know what I'd say to him?'

Ames grinned crookedly.

'Don't make me blush. But Art doesn't have the dough. He doesn't know where it is. You do know where it is?'

'When they help me spring Mel I'll show them. I don't care what Art told you. I made a deal and I'm going to keep my part of it. Team up with them if you must, but I'll still stick to what I set out to do.'

'I didn't say I was going to team up with them. You came to my room last night to ask me to team up with you against them, didn't you?'

'Like I told you, mister. Some nights I have bad dreams. In the daylight I sail along fine.'

'Let's have a gander at another angle, Eve. Supposing — just supposing, mind you — that Mel doesn't make it, or that a snag crops up to prevent us doing the good turn he expects. For how much longer after that do you imagine your boyfriends will be patient with you?'

Her eyes took on a smoky veil.

'What are you trying to spell out, Ames?'

'I'm not sure myself. I haven't really gone into all the details.'

'Save yourself the time and bother,' she said coldly.

Just then Dave Huggins came to the back door to ask her if he could have a spare basin to catch the sump oil. Eve found a plastic basin in the cupboard beside the sink and gave it to him. The man eyed the pair of them warily.

'Learning how to do household chores, Lew?'

'Yeah, I was,' Ames replied. 'I'll go help you finish off what you're doing with the car.'

12

Next morning they were all set to commence the long drive to Blandon. Macklin, with some help from Ames, had mapped out the route they would take. No matter how they calculated, the distance they would have to travel remained in the region of five hundred miles.

'You had it off almost pat,' Macklin commented. 'Are you always so good at guessing?'

'I believe I'm slightly psychic,' Ames told him.

It was Macklin who decided then how they should travel. By his talk he had worked it out for himself, but Ames suspected that he and Huggins had put their heads together over this one.

'I've thought about it carefully,' he announced. 'You and Lew will travel together, Eve, in Ames' car. I'll drive the Olds, and Dave will take the Ford.'

‘Why can’t I drive my own car?’ the woman demanded. And why can’t I travel alone?’

‘I like the way she says it,’ Ames remarked drily. ‘Why can’t she drive on her own? We don’t seem to hit it off too good.’

‘You don’t drive by yourself, Eve,’ Macklin said flatly.

‘Why not?’ she flashed. ‘And don’t say it’s because you don’t trust me. I can’t make a move until we help Mel to escape.’

‘Because I say that you don’t,’ Macklin rasped. ‘And look,’ he went on forcibly, ‘there isn’t much reason for taking you on the trip at all if you’re going to act huffy. You can stay at home here with Dave, and leave Lew and me to swing the rescue attempt.’

‘That’s what you think,’ Eve retorted. ‘I’m going and nobody’s going to hold me back.’

‘Do you want to ride double with Dave?’

‘If there has to be a choice I’ll go with Ames,’ she said with ill grace.

‘Great!’ Huggins grumbled. ‘I must have slipped somewhere along the line since I was known to all the ladies as one of the great lovers of the age.’

‘I know one thing,’ Macklin said angrily. ‘If we go on fighting amongst ourselves like a lot of wildcats it’ll be a miracle if we ever do anything for Mel. Are we straight now?’

Nobody answered him. Macklin continued.

‘So okay. You and Eve hit the road, Lew. Half an hour later Dave will go next. Half an hour after that I’ll leave. Anyplace we stop for a drink or for eats, we’ll stop for no longer than ten minutes. And don’t forget to keep tanked up with fuel. If you have a flat, don’t spend more time than you need to change the wheel. If you develop engine trouble, then you’d better sit where you are until Dave overtakes you.’

‘How about if something happens to your car?’ Ames asked Macklin.

‘Don’t you worry about it. Just get to Blandon. When you do, check into some small hotel. But do it separately, Lew.’

'You think we're going to check in as a honeymoon couple?' Eve sneered. 'Will you be able to find the hotel?'

'I'll find it. Lew, you call yourself Fred Smith. Eve, you check in as Dorothy Chalmers. Is everything clear?'

'Sure,' Ames said.

He had his own suitcase in the trunk of the Dodge and now he had to open the trunk to put Eve's in as well. She stood by him as he did so and spotted the shotgun.

'What do you carry that for?'

'Shooting dames that crawl around in my hair like a bug. If you want to know, I carried it as a front to get lodgings with Dobbs. I said I was keen on a little duck-shooting.'

'I'm not going to enjoy this.'

'You don't have to enjoy it,' he said sharply. 'Far as I can see, you've forgotten how to enjoy anything.'

She flounced off to the passenger seat and settled herself. Macklin came over as Ames was starting the engine.

'You're sure you'll be able to stick to the route?'

'I think so.'

Macklin grinned at Eve who was sitting stiffly on her seat with a cigarette between her lips.

'Have a nice journey, baby.'

Eve didn't answer him or look at him. Macklin muttered something under his breath and slouched away. Ames engaged gear and set off down the track to reach the road.

* * *

An hour later they were rolling along a freeway. There wasn't much traffic in evidence and the needle of the Dodge hovered on a steady sixty-five.

During that hour the woman had chosen to maintain her rather sulky silence. Ames knew a little about women, but not enough to be able to guess at the root cause of her mood. Perhaps it was reaction, he decided. After years of waiting, she was closer to being with Mel Savage again than she had since he'd been picked up in Maytown following the bank raid.

She might be fearful of the deal failing

to go through. She might be wondering about the changes they would discover in each other. She might even be wondering if she was doing the right thing, and that she'd passed up her golden chance when she took off on her own with the money and didn't keep running.

Ames' thoughts returned to the fat man in Parkdale. He was certain that the fat man had been interested in him. He was not blind to the possibility of the fat man still being on his trail. There were only two reasons he could see for the man's interest in him. He was either an agent acting for Milo Farland, or he was an agent acting for Edward Ogden. At the very first opportunity he would check with the chief, when he could eliminate one of the alternatives. Could there be two alternatives? He didn't know, of course, but he didn't see how there could be. Not unless the gang had been bluffing him concerning Farland, and the fifth member of the gang really was operating from a distance to forestall the possibility of a foul-up.

Ames felt a gentle pressure against his

right shoulder and glanced down at the dark head tilted against him. Eve had fallen asleep. The long dark eyelashes resting on the pale skin made a striking contrast. In sleep the features were relaxed, and he was amazed at how beautifully constructed they were. Meeting this woman on the street, no one would ever guess she was a thief and the comrade of men like Macklin and Huggins and Savage.

At noon the sun stood high in a flawless sky. Ames was beginning to feel thirsty and hungry. Eve continued to sleep at his side. When he saw a roadside tavern sign up ahead he slowed and waited for an opening to draw on to the asphalt clearing.

He had switched off the motor before the woman jerked and sat up suddenly, wide-eyed and alert at once.

'Where are we?' she panted. 'Why are we stopping?'

'Take it easy,' he said. 'You're as nervous as six cats. Do you want to attract attention?'

She was looking at the parked cars and

trucks, and understanding caused some of the tension to leave her. She stretched her arms and yawned.

'I do feel hungry, and I need to use a loo.'

'Same here,' Ames grunted. 'You hike to the powder room and I'll go on inside and order.'

She thought about that for a moment, suspicion returning to her eyes. Ames feigned annoyance.

'What's the matter? Do you think I'll take off and leave you?'

'Order me a steak if it's available. Some potatoes.'

'You are hungry,' he smiled. 'If you practised real hard, you might manage to get back to being human.'

'Keep your wisecracks for an audience that'll appreciate them, mister. I was dreaming,' she added wrily.

'Nice going if you can make it. What were you dreaming about — you and me together on a strip of golden sand?'

'Those dogs you told us about. I could see Mel running for the car. Then I heard the dogs. Then I saw the dogs jumping at

Mel. There were so many of them they hid Mel from view. When they finally laid off, Mel had gone. Just vanished into thin air. The — the dogs must have eaten him.'

Ames laughed shortly.

'And you're going to tackle a steak? Get your fanny off that seat, honey and hustle it up. I'll see you inside.'

He watched her make for the conveniences at one side of the building, then he hurried from the car and went into the chrome and tile diner. There were about a dozen customers at the long counter and scattered over the tables. He noticed a phone booth in a corner and headed to it, feeling in his pockets for change.

There was a trucker in the booth and Ames cursed. It was thirty seconds before the trucker finished talking in a loud voice and emerged. He was tall and deep-chested.

'It's all yours, buddy.'

Ames went in and drew the door to. He kept his eyes on the entrance door as he lifted the receiver and began dialling. He had swivelled two numbers when he saw Eve come into the diner. She gazed round the place before her attention swung to the phone booth. By then Ames had replaced the receiver and had lifted the phone book. Eve hurried to the booth and pulled the door open.

'What are you doing?' she cried hoarsely.

'Don't get into a sweat. I was thinking of checking out the best place to stop in Blandon.'

'You won't find Blandon in that book,' she said tautly. 'Also you don't have to find the best place. You heard what Art said.'

Ames shrugged and took her to a table. A waitress in a white coat came over to them and smiled.

'Hi there, kids. What'll it be?'

They ordered and then Ames said he needed to wash his hands. 'I could do with a shower after that heat.'

'They had showers in Blandon?'

'Why do you keep trying to trip me up?'

'Your conscience must be bothering you if you think I am. A man with a clear conscience wouldn't have to worry about being tripped up.'

'Listen,' Ames said. 'Forty-eight hours with you and your sidekicks would turn any guy's head. Do you realize that none of you is normal?'

'I know,' Eve said with a faint smile. 'We are all frustrated. Go wash your hands.'

They took a full twenty minutes over their food. It was well-cooked, and Eve admitted it tasted better than anything she had eaten in months.

'Don't rock your own boat,' Ames grinned. 'There isn't a thing the matter with your cooking.'

'Doesn't it lack inspiration?'

'A hungry man never notices paltry details.'

They were unwinding gradually, and he was convinced that a few days away from Macklin and Huggins and mixing with different people would work wonders on her.

He was offering her a cigarette when the hand holding the pack gave a violent tremor. Eve stared at his face and then followed the direction of his gaze to where a fat man had just entered the diner and was taking one of the stools at the counter.

'Is that him?'

'Yeah,' he said slowly. 'What the hell *is* going on?'

Eve became immediately anxious. Her lips went as white as her cheeks usually were.

'Are you sure it's the same man?'

'Of course I'm sure. Take a hard look at him.'

'It wouldn't matter,' Eve said. 'I've never seem him before in my life.'

'You're sure. I mean, it couldn't be Milo Farland with a little extra weight on?'

'Nobody would mistake him for Milo Farland. He has followed us. Your car is the giveaway. He recognized it.'

Again Ames wondered who the man could be. He had betrayed himself unthinkingly to Eve, as now she would know the man again for herself when she saw him, and would be able to point him out to the others. If he did happen to be a federal agent, that wasn't too good at all.

But surely Ogden would have more sense than to pin such a blatant amateur on to him?

Eve was growing more agitated. She lifted her purse.

'Let's get out of here, Ames.'

'Slow down. If he's so anxious to meet up with me, maybe I ought to take the bull by the horns.'

'And spoil everything, perhaps. No! You can't do it.'

'Want to bet?'

'If you do I'm clearing out. I won't go another yard with you. I'll stay here and wait for Dave or Art.'

The fat man was ordering from the attendant at that moment. Since taking his stool at the counter he hadn't turned his head to look at anybody.

Ames was caught in indecision. If he braced the man and he did turn out to be a comrade, it would create a fuss that he mightn't be able to iron out with Eve. On the other hand, he hated having somebody shadowing him without knowing what was behind it.

'Farland could be playing it smart,' he

said to Eve. 'He could have designs on his share of the loot, and has hired this guy to do the leg work for him.'

'I don't care a damn. I want to get clear of him.'

'What else could he be?' Ames murmured.

'Surely you can make one more guess,' Eve said vehemently. 'Someone who has followed you from the prison farm. It's what came to my mind when you mentioned it at the beginning. I just knew it!' she groaned. 'It was all too good to be true. There had to be a string.'

'Pull yourself together. All right, we'll simply beat it. Get going.'

The fat man was busy with a knife and fork as they walked to the door of the diner and passed into the sunshine.

'I meant to buy a few cans of beer,' Ames said.

'You can buy them someplace else. Get into the car and drive like blazes.'

'No,' Ames said thoughtfully.

'What do you mean, no?' Eve panted. 'I've got raps hanging over me, even if you haven't.'

'We'll wait for a few minutes and see if he comes out.'

'What then?' the woman asked harshly.

'If he does show I'll brace him.'

'Count me out. I'm not going to stand around and watch you flex your muscles.'

They walked towards the Dodge, but then Ames halted and scanned the cars that were parked.

'That old Plymouth wasn't there when he arrived. You get into our heap and I'll take a look at the registration tag.'

'You can think fast when you want to, Ames. Okay. It might tell you something. But what if he comes out and finds you poking in his car?'

Ames left her without answering. The Plymouth had been driven into a slot between two trucks. He ducked round the back of the nearest one and approached the driving side of the Plymouth.

The fat man hadn't bothered to lock the door and Ames plucked it open and leaned over the steering column. The car was registered in the name of Harold J. Good, and Good's address was Pollock Avenue, Blandon.

He wasn't an agent at all then. He had started out from Blandon and now he was working round to home again. Coincidence? No, it wasn't coincidence. Somehow or other, this was tied up with the prison farm. As Eve had feared, a tail had been put on him when he left the farm and had remained with him since.

Ames went cold when he realized what this actually meant. He had been followed from the prison farm to Delton City. The fat man would have followed him around Delton City. He would be dumb if he couldn't manage to put one and one together in this context.

The fat man must know who he was.

He heard the door of the diner slapping and back-tracked to the rear of the truck. Going round it he glimpsed the fat man walking quickly to the Plymouth. A lot of thoughts raced through Ames' mind at that instant. He should have heeded Edward Ogden. He should have agreed to another agent taking over and stepping into his shoes. The chief should be informed at once of the course events were taking.

Why was Harold Good interested in him? Why, why, why?

Eve was sitting behind the wheel of the Dodge when he joined her. When he frowned his surprise she merely switched on the motor.

'Let me handle this for a while. Did you see him leave the diner?'

'Yeah, I did.' Ames got in beside her. 'You're much too nervous to drive. I'm in no great hurry to get to heaven.'

'You just imagine you can drive. I'll give him and his heap something to keep them busy.'

With that she edged off the asphalt, paused for an opening to cut across the freeway, then she rammed her foot at the gas pedal and the Dodge leaped forward.

Ames adjusted the driving mirror to watch the traffic surging in the lane behind them. He kept squinting for sign of another car leaving the forecourt of the diner. If Good was intent on keeping them in sight then it was time he was on the move again. But did he have to strain himself to remain in touch? Did he not know by now where Ames' ultimate destination lay?

Sweat rose to his brow as the truth filtered through to him. Yes, the fat man did know where he was headed. He knew Ames would finish up in Blandon. Did it mean that something was building up to crash down on the plan he had laboured on?

'Can you see him?' Eve asked. She was taking everything out of the Dodge it was capable of.

'No, I can't see him. And slow it up a little, will you. According to the map, we've got to leave the freeway pretty soon.'

'I can read a map as well as you,' the woman said. 'I can recognize the place where we turn off. I mean to give that tub of lard a run for it. Did you read the registration sticker?'

'No. He surprised me just as I was about to close in on his car.'

Eve threw him a glance that was both dubious and appraising. She switched her eyes to the road ahead and passed a foreign sports car with mere inches to spare.

Ames slumped back on his seat and fumbled for a cigarette.

13

In the late afternoon they halted at a roadhouse for another meal. Eve had driven for most of the afternoon, and there were little lines of strain and weariness settling on her forehead and between her eyes.

'I could sleep for a week,' she announced to Ames while they were eating. 'Why didn't you get in some sleeping when I was driving? Then you'd be fresh for tonight.'

'I couldn't relax,' Ames replied. 'I was afraid of you making a wrong turning somewhere. Anyhow, who says we're going to keep rolling all night?'

'Look, mister, you heard what Art said. We move and we keep moving until we hit Blandon.'

'Do you think Dave and Art will make it a non-stop effort? Not a chance. With a co-driver you can keep driving until a car gives up, but one man tires no matter how tough he is.'

Ames was hoping for an opportunity to get in touch with Edward Ogden and report in on Harold Good. Failing to manage that, he was anxious to have a look at a phone book covering Blandon. If Good was a tradesman or a professional man, it would say so in the directory. Whatever Good was, the phone book might provide a clue as to his reason for following Ames.

Insurance sprang to his mind, and he couldn't dismiss this lightly. If Good had set out from Blandon, it indicated his release from the prison farm having activated a switch to set the fat man in motion.

Ames explored the possibilities of the prison farm itself. He was pretty certain he had played a convincing role as a prisoner. All the same, there were cunning men at that place. Burt Lashley was fox-crafty as well as a hopeless sadist.

There was Jules Colport to consider, also.

These men knew why Mel Savage was in prison; they knew that the quarter million dollars which Savage's gang had stolen had never been recovered.

Then there was the hospital episode. Perhaps Wilf Fletcher hadn't played his part well enough, or perhaps he had over-played it by keeping him in sick bay against Colport's wishes. Suspicions could have been aroused that in turn could have triggered off a chain reaction.

There was another angle to consider.

It was possible that someone in authority at the prison farm, realizing that Ames and Savage were too pally for words, had set about drawing his own conclusions. He might see it this way: Savage had been plotting something between them, something that had to do with the bank haul, or the gang that Savage had run with. So how to discover what the plot comprised? The obvious answer would be to put a tail on Ames and keep it pinned to him until light began to throw up some facts in relief.

'That guy has got you worried,' Eve was saying to him. They had finished eating and were smoking cigarettes.

Outside, the sun was slipping from the

sky. The roadhouse was beginning to come to life for the evening. Cars kept arriving at short intervals and couples came in — mostly young and carefree, and wrapped up in each other to the exclusion of the rest of the world.

Eve's gaze followed such a couple to a table in a shadowy corner. The girl was blonde, perfectly tanned, and with attractive features and limbs. Her companion was dark and slim, and pulsating with animal energy. They sat down and the young man leaned over to steal a kiss. They kissed and giggled.

'Ugh!' Ames said.

'What's the matter with you?'

'Those kids necking. Why do they have to make such an exhibition of their appetities?'

'You're going sour, man. That or you're growing old.'

'Am I?' Ames met the cool dark eyes and grinned. 'What were you saying?'

'That fat guy.'

'Yeah. I admit he's got me bugged. But he looks harmless enough from a distance.'

‘So does a knife,’ Eve said thinly. ‘It isn’t so harmless when somebody’s ramming it into your back.’

There was no opportunity to use the phone here either. It seemed that Eve had decided she must not let him out of her sight for longer than a few minutes at a time. Had Macklin drilled this into her before they set off?

They went out to the parking area and Ames looked around for the Plymouth. He saw no sign of it and joined Eve in the Dodge. Now it was he who took over the wheel.

‘You didn’t see his car?’

Ames shook his head.

‘I guess we were travelling too fast for him.’

‘If we keep going we might shake his off.’

‘You wouldn’t rather wait for Art to get this length and tell him about the fat guy?’

‘That wouldn’t help matters. No, we keep driving, mister.’

She fell asleep almost as soon as they hit the road. As before, her head tilted over to his shoulder. The pale features relaxed and she sighed in her sleep.

To follow the route they had planned, it was necessary at times to leave the highway and travel on secondary roads. This was the part Ames liked least, as there were so many intersections, and so many of these inadequately signposted. Also, the roads were much narrower, with enough bends to keep him straining for alertness.

The night was a dark one, starless, and with heavy clouds bulking low on the hills they were travelling through. At midnight Ames had had enough and halted at a small motel. Eve jerked awake at once and stared at him.

'What's the big idea?'

'There's no sense in punishing ourselves and the car to death. I'm bushed. I'm not driving another yard until dawn.'

'Then I'll drive,' Eve said coldly.

'Can you find the direction in the dark?'

'You mean we're lost?' she cried in dismay.

'I figure we might be. In any case,

there's no great hurry. We're well in front of Dave and Art. We'll put up here, get a meal, and have a decent rest.'

Her eyes glittered on the sprawling motel units. A faint light glowed in the reception office, but the office was empty. She gazed on to the front of the restaurant, her mouth tightening up.

'I'll go in there and ask for direction to Blandon. You can sleep while I drive the rest of the way.'

'Nothing doing,' Ames said stubbornly. 'If you make it on to Blandon tonight, you walk or you bum a ride, but you don't drive my car.'

'What the hell has gotten into you?'

'Nothing.' He relented. 'Look, Eve, try and be human for a change — '

'What do you mean — human?' she said harshly. 'Drop that human stuff, will you. I don't like you, Ames. I don't trust you.'

'You were dreaming again.'

'Never mind what I was doing.' She sat still and sulked for a moment. Ames extracted the ignition key from the socket and climbed out.

'Come on,' he said.

She didn't answer him. She didn't even look at him, but kept her pale face averted. Ames shrugged and headed for the reception office. He hadn't gone far when he heard feet running after him.

'Art's not going to like this when I tell him.'

'Who's worrying about Art? Are you worrying about Art? Is Art worrying about you?'

'I don't like it either.'

'But then you have to be careful not to step out of character. What *do* you like?'

The door of the office wasn't locked. Ames pushed it open and walked in to halt at a long desk. There was a sign on the desk beside a bell push which read, 'Ring for Service.'

'Let's get out of here, Lew.'

It was the first time she had used his name and he smiled crookedly at her.

'Hold my hand if you want to.'

He hit the bell push a couple of times. He lit a cigarette while he waited. Presently a stout, bald man bustled into the office and went round the desk. He was mopping his brow with a handkerchief.

'Sorry I was out,' he apologized. 'Would you believe it,' he went on happily. 'I got a full house tonight.'

Eve gripped Ames' fingers and tugged.

'There you are. We're out of luck. Well drive on and find some other place.' Her voice was thick with relief.

'Oh, no,' the stout man said. 'Not quite full. I've got one apartment left.'

Eve's fingernails gouged into the palm of Ames' hand.

'Is it a double?' Ames said.

'Sure is. What a break for you, people. Want to come and look before you make up your mind?'

'It doesn't matter,' Ames told him. 'We'll buy it.' He heard Eve groaning at his back.

'You cheap chiseller!' she whispered.

'What does your wife say, sir?'

'She's just tired,' Ames told him.

The man produced registration cards and stated his rates. 'You'll find it's a lot cheaper by the week.'

'We're staying for the night only.'

He signed as Mr and Mrs Fred Smith. He paid and the man found a key. At the door he waited for Ames and Eve to precede him outside. He followed them and pointed to a parking lot.

'You can leave your car there or park it opposite the apartment. We don't mind which.'

He took them along a gravel walk, past the units squatting side by side like so many upturned boxes. Laughter drifted out of one of them. In another a woman was screaming furiously.

'I'll really have to call with the Jordans,' the stout man said apologetically. 'They're sure lowering the tone of the place.'

He halted at number twenty and inserted the key in the door, excusing himself to go in before them to switch on the lights. The boxes weren't so bad inside, Ames saw. They were shown the roomy lounge, the twin bedrooms, the tiny bathroom and the equally tiny kitchen.

'Some folks like to do their own cooking. We don't mind at all. Still, the chef in our restaurant is second to none.'

'We'll try him in the morning,' Ames said.

He thanked the stout man and he left them. Eve stood in the centre of the lounge and gathered up her hands into fists.

'What the hell are you trying to prove?' she demanded.

'Prove? What do I have to prove? I'm tired and you're tired. We'll have a long rest and be fresh to hit the road in the morning. Do you feel hungry?'

She shook her head slowly.

'I'm just mad, mister. Mad clear through. How are you going to explain this to Art?'

'I don't have to explain anything to Art. And if you imagine I'm setting up something that I can brag about later, then you're crazy. Who wants to seduce an iceberg? Not me, lady. I like my women warm and tender.'

'You bastard,' she said with soft venom.

'Okay, okay. Go freshen up. Then go to bed. I'm going to bring the car over, and I might bring a bottle while I'm at it.'

He left her on that note, walking back

along the gravel path to the restaurant. The bar was closed, he learned. There would be no drinks until the morning, a waiter told him. But if he wanted refeshment that badly he might be able to strain a point.

'Then strain it.' Ames said and gave him the price of a bottle of scotch together with an extra dollar.

With the bottle under his arm he left the restaurant and went on to collect the Dodge. He drove it in close to the unit and made sure all the doors were locked before leaving it.

Eve was sitting on an easy chair, a cigarette in her lips and a faraway look in her eyes. She ignored the drink that Ames poured for her. He took a drink himself, then pulled off his jacket and tie and went to the bathroom.

Eve was still where he'd left her when he emerged. But he noticed she'd drunk a little of the whisky.

'Which of the bedrooms do you fancy?'

She didn't answer him. He shrugged, tossing the ignition key of the Dodge in his hand.

He took the first bedroom off the lounge, looking longingly at the turned-down bed. He had forgotten the suitcases, he realized and went out to the car again to collect them. He left Eve's on the lounge floor and returned to the bedroom with his own. He stripped and drew on his pyjamas. He sat on the edge of the bed and smoked a cigarette. He smoked it half-way down and mashed it into a bowl. Then he switched off the light and lay down on the bed.

* * *

He awakened and thought he was back at the prison farm. In his sleep Mel Savage had been leaning over his bunk and nudging at his shoulder. Mel's sweaty face had been thrust close to his own.

'*You've got to get me out of here, Lew. You've got to get me out . . .*'

The words faded from his conscious mind. The room might be dark, but it wasn't packed with groaning, squirming, nightmare-racked bodies. The air was clean enough and he had a room all to himself. Or had he?

He felt that something had brought him awake, something quite apart from the bad dream. He was lifting himself up on his elbow when he became aware of a slight draught blowing on his face from the direction of the bedroom door.

Alarmed, he stretched out a hand to the bedside lamp and jerked the cord.

Eve Birchall was standing just inside the doorway. She was wearing nothing but pink, frilly pyjamas. Her thick hair was brushed out about her slim shoulders in a dark mass, making a striking frame for the paleness of her face and her oddly luminous eyes.

'You gave me a fright then,' Ames grunted. He frowned when she just stood there and stared at him. 'Say, is something the matter with you?'

'I couldn't sleep. I guess I slept too long in the car.'

'And you were having another bad dream? Don't let it throw you, Eve. So was I. I thought I was back in that prison farm.'

He fancied a shudder ran through her

body. Concerned, he flung the bedclothes back and poked in the suitcase for his robe.

'Here, put this on.'

She allowed him to drape the robe around her, but then, for some reason, she tugged the robe off and flung it to the floor. Ames ran his fingers through his hair in perplexity.

'Okay. Have another huff if you want to. How about a drink to mellow you down?'

'I don't want a drink.'

'Then what the hell do you want?'

She was staring at him as he said that and he caught a quick tremor of her lower lip. His eyes rivetted on those lips. They weren't tightened in on themselves any longer. They were full and blossoming, like rosebuds reaching to the sun.

His eyes shifted from her mouth to her face, to the delicately moulded cheeks, the fragile chin. Lastly they lifted on to Eve's eyes.

Understanding hit him like a thunderbolt.

He opened his arms and she moved

into them with a strangled moan coming from her throat.

'I didn't want to do it,' she whispered. 'I — '

He cut off her words with his mouth. The lips were warm and moist and hungry, and the surge of released feeling in Eve caused her to lose balance so that he had to hold her all the more closely to him. His fingers worked at her pyjamas top.

'Put the lamp off,' she mumbled.

'In a minute.'

'Do it now, Lew.'

'You want to think of Mel Savage,' he accused.

She drew her head back and glared angrily at him.

'You're wrong. I'm not thinking of Mel. I'm trying hard not to think of him.'

'So you don't want to look at me. But I want to look at you.'

Her cheeks flamed and she averted her gaze. He stripped the pyjamas top from her and let it fall to the floor. Her breasts were rich and full and firm, the skin soft as silk to the touch.

'You're a wonderful woman, Eve,' Ames murmured.

'So we stand here while you pass comments on my body?'

'We'll go into all that later,' he told her. He stretched over and switched the lamp off, then led her towards his bed.

* * *

It was well after dawn when they woke. Ames came awake first and was moving carefully over the floor when the woman stirred and opened her eyes. He saw brief panic flare in them.

'Where are you going?'

'To have a shower. Don't worry,' he grinned. 'I'm not going to take off naked as the day I was born.'

'You look splendid naked, Lew.'

'You too, baby.' He went back and kissed her on the mouth. She would have drawn him down beside her if he hadn't broken free and stood up.

'Hey there! Easy does it. We've got to get dressed, eat, and clear out of this joint. A whole night has gone past, remember.'

She nodded, not saying anything. A

shadow crossed her features as events slid into perspective.

Ames' own thoughts were in turmoil as he showered, shaved, and came back to dress. He had taken the woman lightly, and now he saw there was far more to her than he'd ever realized. He was a fool to have complicated matters. Eve wasn't just a casual pickup. She didn't go for a man and then forget him. But the hell with it. It was she who had thrown herself at him, and not the other way round. But even this attitude didn't make him feel any easier.

They packed their suitcases and Ames stowed them in the trunk of the Dodge. Then they cruised down to the restaurant for breakfast. There was no sign of the fat man's Plymouth. No sign either of the Ford or the Oldsmobile.

Directly after breakfast they left the motel and continued on their journey to Blandon.

14

It was as though Eve had opened a door to her deepest feelings and her most secret thoughts, and then decided to close it again. She became moody, taciturn. When he spoke to her she answered in monosyllables or not at all. He suspected she was regretting what had happened last night. Well, let her regret all she wanted to. He had not done anything she wasn't in agreement with. Still, he couldn't help wondering at the real reason for her change of attitude.

'So you just want to forget it,' he said after a while.

He had roused her from some other avenue of thought, and she turned her head to stare blankly for a moment.

'That's right,' she said vaguely.

'What's right. You do or you don't.'

'You're confusing me, Ames. You'd better keep your eyes on the road.'

It was a long time after this when she

gave vent to a laugh that startled him.

'What's so funny?'

'I was thinking of you and me getting married.'

'Carry on laughing,' Ames told her. 'That isn't only funny. It's uproarious.'

'You wouldn't like to get married?'

'Is that a proposal?'

'Were you ever married?'

'I never will be, if I can help it.'

'You guys are all the same,' she said bitterly. 'Taking what you want and not giving anything in exchange.'

'Look, Eve, are you going to go philosophic on me?'

'Shut your damn mouth,' she said.

They arrived in Blandon at last. There was a dark sky hanging over the town and the sky was pumping rain furiously. Ames stopped at the first restaurant he saw, where they went in and had a substantial meal.

Back in the Dodge they drove around to find a hotel to suit them. Blandon was like a score of other medium-sized towns that Ames had been in. With the rain on it looked bleak and dismal, but it mightn't look so bad when the sun came out.

'Which road would you take to get at the prison farm?'

'I'm not perfectly certain,' he replied to Eve's question.

'But you've been there . . . '

'Of course I've been there. But I never hit this town on my wanderings. Soon as I got out of the farm I kept going like blazes away from it.'

'Poor Mel,' she said.

'Poor Mel. Look, let's find the kind of joint that Art would expect us to look in at.'

'Then we could take a drive and find the road leading to the farm?' she suggested.

'You can't wait to find it. You can't wait until you find Mel. Have you ever thought that you might be disappointed?'

Her eyes clouded furiously.

'Don't give me that. You might be a woman's dream in bed, but it doesn't start and finish in bed.'

'You mentioned marriage.'

'I'm going to marry Mel.'

'Would you marry me instead if I asked you?'

Her eyes narrowed now.

'I smell a rat, mister. This rat has a yen to feed on a pile of the long green stuff. A quarter-million dollars worth.'

'It makes my head swim. And you figure you've got my motives weighed up, don't you? Say we did hit it off, though. Would we share and share alike?'

'You're forgetting Art and Dave.'

'I'm not forgetting anything. But if you and Mel would be capable of taking off and leaving them in the lurch, then why not apply that to you and me?'

'You've got a twisted brain, Ames. Do you see everything in terms of putting one over on your neighbour?'

'Not at all. But I'll tell you something. If Art and Dave get their hands on the dough, then they'll have no qualms over leaving you and Mel out in the cold.'

She looked at him squarely.

'Exactly what are you driving at? Are you really putting a proposition to me?'

'You might not have the dough at all.'

She laughed, but it was a laugh without mirth. He judged the emotions that contributed to the eruption and found them solidly based and confident. This woman knew where the money was, without doubt. She could lead him to it at any time. She was supremely satisfied regarding its safety.

They found a hotel and booked in. Ames had told Eve he would try and get a room on the third floor. She should do the same. Business was so slack at the hotel he could have had a room on any of the five floors. He ran the Dodge into the basement garage, leaving Eve to walk about for a few minutes. He was given room 310 and Eve was given 318.

Ames waited for fifteen minutes before going to her door and tapping on it. Inside, he wanted to take her into his arms, but Eve fended him off.

'Do you want Art or Dave to walk in on us?' she reasoned.

'It isn't Art or Dave you're worried about, baby. It's Mel, isn't it?'

'And why the hell shouldn't it be? Oh, Lew, try and be a sport. I want to get Mel out of that place. I must concentrate on nothing else until it's over. If I allow myself to be sidetracked, I'll never forgive myself.'

'I didn't realize I had so much charm.'

'Wipe that silly grin off your face. You have it, mister, and I go for it. But I've carried this torch for too long to drop it at this stage of the game.'

Ames left her and went back to his own room. At least he had allayed whatever suspicions she had been harbouring concerning his background and motives. A few minutes later he opened the room door and looked out along the passage. There was no one in sight and he started walking quickly to the elevator.

In the lobby, he went on to the street, seeing that the rain had passed and the heavy clouds were breaking up. He didn't go far from the hotel, as he didn't want to remain away too long, in case Eve decided to pay a call at his room. He found a drug-store that would suit his purpose. There was a phone booth, with a local directory on the stand. He shut himself in the booth and began searching in the book for Harold Good's name.

He didn't find it in the ordinary listings and flipped through to the yellow pages. What trade or profession would a man like Good follow? There was an extremely stupid question. People didn't fit into pigeonholes so easily.

Ames was fumbling for a cigarette when he had an inspiration. A private investigator? Well, wasn't it possible? It was a cinch that Good was investigating him.

He caught his breath when he discovered Good's name under the private detective heading. There was the Pollock Avenue address. Harold J. Good was a private investigator. But why had he tagged on to Lew Ames? Better still, who was paying his tab?

Milo Farland seemed the most logical answer. Farland was in Blandon, and he knew that Mel Savage was a prisoner out at the farm. But granting this much, how had Farland discovered the link between Mel Savage and Lew Ames?

There was yet another point he must consider now. If Harold Good was operating on Milo Farland's behalf and sending in progress reports on him, it followed that Farland might know of Lew Ames being a government agent.

Ames cuffed sweat from his brow.

He lifted the telephone receiver and dialled the Delton City number. A girl answered the call and asked him who he was.

'Lew Ames. Put me on with the chief.'

A short time later he was speaking with Edward Ogden.

'Listen,' he said. 'I'm in Blandon with the woman. The other two characters are on the way. The snatch is going to be set up anytime.'

'I see. Then it's going nicely, Lew. But what's the trouble?'

Ames explained about the fat man's interest in him. He emphasized that Harold Good really knew how to do his job, and that if he was operating for Milo Farland, then there could be dangerous snags ahead.

'Why would he be operating for Farland, Lew?'

'I don't know, sir. I'm simply guessing, of course. But it's a perfectly reasonable deduction to make.'

'Then you need help.'

'Not direct help. I might not require

any at all. If I can get the opportunity to visit with Good at his office — '

'No,' Ogden cut in on him. 'That sounds too risky. I've got a man in Blandon, as it happens.'

'He'll take care of Good?'

'Leave him to me, Lew. Another slant has just occurred to me.'

'Oh. Could you tell me what it is?'

'It wouldn't make you feel any more comfortable. Just carry on and leave this guy to me. I'll put out a tracer for Farland. There's enough stuff on him to hold him.'

'You know what you're doing, I guess.'

'I think so,' the chief said coolly. He said goodbye and hung up.

Ames went back to the hotel. He had been in his room for only a few minutes when the door was rapped. He opened it and saw Art Macklin standing there. Macklin pushed past him into the room. He was displeased about something, Ames saw. He assumed that Macklin had called on Eve first of all and that Eve had told him of the fat man.

'Where were you?' Macklin asked him.

'Eve thought you were in here, but you weren't.'

'I was stiff from so much driving. I took a walk.'

'Your orders were to stay put until you heard from us.'

'What's with this orders gag?' Ames retorted sharply. 'Did somebody give you promotion?'

Macklin's jaw darkened and his blue eyes glittered angrily. Then he had himself in hand. He went over to a chair and slumped down on it. He brought a cigar stub from his jacket and flicked a lighter under it.

'I saw Eve,' he said slowly. 'She was telling me about this fat guy. Why should he be so interested in you?'

Ames shrugged.

'I can't say. I wish I could. Twice might have been a coincidence, but not the third time. Did Eve describe him?'

'Yeah, she did. It didn't make a picture I understand. I'm thinking of Milo . . . '

'So was I,' Ames said. 'This guy could be a good friend. Milo might have designs on the loot after all.'

Macklin had been thinking it over deeply. He shook his head.

'I can't make it fit. If the fat guy was following you around, it says he picked you up because you were in prison with Mel.'

'Sure. And the obvious question stemming from that is, how did he know I was friendly with Mel?'

'Somebody at the prison camp,' Macklin hazarded.

'I can't make that fit,' Ames said. 'But I wouldn't lose too much sleep over him. As I said to Eve, he's only one man, and if he does attempt to throw a spanner in the works we can handle him.'

Macklin puffed gently at his cigar and considered him.

'It's what I've been telling myself. All right, Lew, here's what we've planned. Tomorrow you and I will leave Blandon in time to reach the road above the prison farm at noon.'

'What about Eve and Dave?'

'Forget them for the moment. Like I said earlier, I'm not so sure that Eve is to be trusted. Dave will keep an eye on her.

It would be silly for the four of us to drive out there. It might attract attention from the cops. Eve says you haven't got a clear idea of the road from town.'

'It won't be hard to find out.'

'I've already found out,' Macklin said. He rose from the chair and dropped his cigar stub to the floor. He squashed it under his heel. 'I'll call for you tomorrow morning at eleven.'

'Where are you and Dave staying?'

'At a dump not far from here.'

'What did Eve say when you told her she wasn't driving out to see the prison farm?'

'She didn't mind much. She's growing nervous. Which brings me to something else, Lew. See she doesn't skip the hotel.'

Ames couldn't see Eve skipping anywhere until they had made a try to rescue Savage, and he said so.

'I guess you're right. But get one thing into your head, Lew. She's the key to the dough and not Mel.'

'If she was willing to divvy the proceeds, you wouldn't strain yourself for Mel?'

'I didn't say so,' Macklin snapped sharply. He started for the door. 'Be ready at eleven. Be out on the street where I can pick you up easily. We mustn't forget this fat guy.'

Ames saw Eve in her room later on in the day. She asked him not to stay with her in case Huggins or Macklin was hanging about the hotel. He invited her to eat out somewhere with him and she agreed to this.

They went to a night spot, had dinner and spent an hour dancing. Eve had dug up a dark blue evening frock and she looked stunning in it. While they danced Ames held her close, and he was surprised when she kissed his chin impulsively.

'What was that for?'

'Never mind,' she said. 'But you were right about me forgetting how to be human.'

'I could teach you a lot, baby.'

'Don't get too ambitious, stranger. You could teach me things it would take quite a while to unlearn.'

'And of course there's Mel waiting in the wings.'

'I gave him my promise.'

'You're not such a bad kid at all, Eve.'

She lifted her head swiftly to stare at him, her lips parting slightly in puzzlement.

'That was an odd thing for you to say, Lew.'

'Odd?'

'There's something about you I don't understand. Whenever I think too hard about you I get scared.'

'We could fall for each other, honey,' he said lightly.

'I'm not so sure. You keep striking false notes. And occasionally — Oh, hell, let it drift, Lew.'

'Sure,' Ames murmured. 'Let it drift.'

Taking her back to the hotel in the Dodge he suggested going to her room later.

'We might never get another chance,' he added.

'Cut out that sentimental stuff too. No, we're not going to risk it. Dave and Art have got eyes in the backs of their heads.'

They entered the hotel separately. If Huggins or Macklin was bent on keeping them under surveillance, there was no sign of either of them.

Ames slept soundly that night. He called room service and had his breakfast sent up. A half hour later he went along to Eve's room and was admitted. She had been awake since dawn, she told him. She wished Art had agreed to her going along with them to the road above the prison farm.

'There really isn't much sense in it,' he told her. 'You'll see Mel soon enough. By midnight tomorrow you might be together again.'

'I'm not so sure, Lew. I've got this damned awful feeling.'

'You're always getting them. Why not have a look at the bright side for a change? You'll get old long before your time.'

'I guess you're right.' She relented and smiled. She drew him to her and kissed him on the mouth. 'It's a pity we didn't get together years ago, Lew.'

He decided to make one last throw of the dice.

He gripped her arms and looked into

her face. 'It still isn't too late to make a deal.'

'What — what kind of deal?' she stammered, at the same time aware of what he was driving at.

'Jack this up. Art and Dave and Mel. We'll head for the place where you've stashed the money. Not in an hour's time. Not in a half-hour's time. But right this minute. Then we'll flip the country and really have a ball.'

She hesitated, closing her eyes and bringing her lips tightly together in fierce concentration. A shudder ran through her body and she pushed him away from her.

'No,' she panted hoarsely. 'No! Don't ask me again. If you do, I'm liable to tell Art all about it.'

'Just forget it,' he said, mustering a faint smile. 'You want it your way and your way it's going to be.'

He turned for the door and had reached it when she spoke at his back.

'Please try to understand me, Lew.'

'Sure I'll try. See you later, baby.'

At five minutes before eleven he rode down in the elevator and crossed the lobby to the street. The first thing he saw was Dave Huggins in the dark green Ford. Huggins was parked on the opposite side of the street, with a newspaper draped over the steering wheel. Even as his eyes found Huggins, the swarthy man looked at him. He gave no sign of recognition, but dropped his head to his newspaper.

Ames heard a car moving from the far end of the street. It was the big Olds, and when it drew level with Ames it halted. Ames gripped the door handle and opened it. He settled down beside Macklin and slammed the door. The Olds went into motion, Macklin glancing at the Ford to incline his head to the watching Huggins.

'Dave is going to keep tabs on Eve?'

'Yeah,' Macklin grunted. 'That's right. You and she are worth watching, chum.' He gave a hard, mirthless laugh and tooled the big car on out of the street.

15

They were well on their way to the outskirts of Blandon before Ames replied to Macklin's remark. His first reaction was to ignore the crack, treating it as Macklin obviously meant him to treat it. But then he wasn't so sure. He had the feeling that the crook intended to thrust a barb under his skin. If he didn't make some response Macklin would get the idea he was on to something, when his suspicion would increase in dimension.

'What did you mean by that, Art?'

Macklin was watching the thick traffic and driving with the utmost care so as not to attract the wrong sort of attention. He had an unlit cigarette between his lips and was working it from one side of his mouth to the other. He threw a sharp glance at his passenger, one eyebrow lifting quizzically.

'What do I mean by what?' he said, evidently having forgotten what he had said.

'About Eve and me.'

'Eve and you!' Macklin's laugh was a gusty explosion. 'I don't know. I was just shooting in the dark.'

Ames was reluctant to believe this. Perhaps Macklin or Huggins had seen Eve and him together last night. Perhaps the crook really was shooting in the dark, for the sake of seeing what would happen if Ames got hit in a tender place.

'Well, point your gun at somebody else,' he said.

'Okay, okay, Lew. Don't be so cursed touchy.'

'I'm not touchy. But everyone else in this outfit is.'

'Let's drop it.'

Ames lit a cigarette for himself and watched the last buildings on the fringe of Blandon fade from sight. Ahead of them lay a section of rolling hills; the upper part of their slopes was wooded and the tops of the trees looked like green carpet in the early sunlight. He looked back and down on Blandon. It was little more than a toytown now, with the people in it not real people at all, but tiny, insignificant specks. His thoughts drifted to Eve Birchall.

He was pretty certain that it wouldn't take much more pressure to be exerted on Eve before she would give in to him, quit the whole game she had been involved in, and go away with him to unearth the quarter million dollars.

As Ames saw it, that would be the ideal solution. They wouldn't have to spring Savage from the prison farm at all. All that was required to spoil the escape was a phone call. It could be an anonymous one and no one at the farm would be any the wiser.

As for Huggins and Macklin, another phone call would have them picked up inside twenty-four hours. With Savage in prison, and Farland in the process of being traced and pulled in, the arrest of the two men would mean the end of the gang. Eve would show him where the money was hidden, and when she did, he would tell her who he really was and take her in also.

Viewing it dispassionately, it seemed it could all be pulled off simply enough.

And a few months ago he could have gone through each of the necessary motions without thinking beyond the purely mechanical action. The complexion of the affair had altered considerably. Eve Birchall wasn't merely a confederate of gangsters. She was, first of all, a human being; after that she became a woman in his estimation, a woman whom, in different circumstances, he might have fallen in love with and married.

He tried to tell himself he was growing soft, that the year at the prison farm had made mush of his brains. He knew it wasn't so. He knew he was ready to grasp at any explanation if he could utilize it to justify the pattern his behaviour must take in the near future.

He knew he had put all the pressure on Eve that it would be sensible to apply. She would lean over so far with him, but she had set and recognised a limit. Perhaps she worried about what her conscience might do to her afterwards. Or it might be the physical menace of Savage himself which provided the deterrent. Or, deep down in her, she might really love Mel

Savage as she had never loved any other man, and it was this love which motivated her in the final analysis.

Macklin was driving through open country now. They had climbed into the hills and the hills had started to dwindle and merge with thousands of acres of farmland. The crook appeared to have a pretty good idea of direction, and this prodded Ames to asking him if he'd made a practice run already.

'No, I haven't. But I obtained clear instruction. We should be hitting a crossroads soon. Keep your eyes peeled. We take the left fork.'

They came to the crossroads presently, and the character of the country became such that Ames was certain he recognized it.

'We must be drawing close to the prison farm,' he announced a few moments later.

Macklin gave him an appraising stare, and he judged that this was where the crook would finally reach a decision concerning the truth of the story Ames had told them.

'How do you know?' he asked Ames.

'The trees down there.' Ames pointed. 'I know they're the same trees. And this is the road we used to look at.'

'You got a feeling for the place, huh?'

'I sure have,' Ames replied with a soberness that impressed Macklin. 'Look, slow up or we'll drift past before you realize it. It can't be far from here to where you'll be able to look down at the fields and the compound. Oh, hell!' he exploded suddenly.

'What's wrong?' Macklin demanded.

'We should have brought glasses.'

'I brought them,' Macklin told him and smiled sourly. 'It takes one clear head at least for a gag like this.'

They hadn't met much traffic since leaving the road fork a mile or so back, but now, as they slowed almost to a standstill, Ames heard a car trundling in the distance behind them. He jerked his head to peer through the window.

'Don't act scared,' Macklin warned. 'Behave normally.'

'I am behaving normally. I'm sweating. The prison authorities might have this road patrolled.'

‘Or that fat guy could be after you again. I wonder who he is.’

The vehicle coming up behind them wasn’t a car at all, but an old jeep, with a man in overalls at the wheel. The jeep and the man reminded Ames of Jack Dobbs. There was ample room for the jeep to pass, which it did as the two men looked casually at it. The driver had a pipe in his mouth and raised his hand.

‘Hi, granddad,’ Macklin murmured. ‘I bet he takes us for officials from the prison.’

The jeep had gone on and now Ames was peering over the trees in order to get a glimpse of the fields where the prisoners would be labouring. He looked at his wristwatch, noting the time was five minutes to noon.

‘You’ve stopped short. A hundred yards or so, and the whole layout should be clear.’

Macklin cast him another keen glance but said nothing. He drove slowly forward. There seemed to be nothing but trees, and Ames was wondering if he had made a mistake when they cleared suddenly and the patchwork of fields became visible, with the dim outline of the compound buildings beyond.

They sat and watched the ant-like creatures working in the fields. Ames saw a truck describe a circle behind the workers. It unloaded topsoil and then went on to the heap of rocks and rubble.

'What's happening?' Macklin asked him.

'The trucks come in with soil from land being cleared for building projects. Then they load up with the rocks the prisoners are ripping from the ground.'

'What do they use the rocks for?'

'Foundations. It's good stuff for bottoming roads so they won't sink.'

'Why the hell don't they use bulldozers and grabbers for clearing the rocks?'

'You ought to take it up with Jules Colport,' Ames suggested. 'His idea is that the prisoners need the fresh air and exercise.'

'I'd go crazy in a week, Lew.'

'You might not, Art. Fresh air is great stuff. So is hard work. You can develop a rhythm that takes over your system. It's okay if you don't worry too much.'

'You can have it, chum,' Macklin growled. 'My share of it as well.' He lifted a set of powerful binoculars and put them to his eyes. He focused them carefully.

'How is it coming through?'

Macklin didn't answer him. He was allowing the lenses to rove over the ant-like creatures.

'There's a bastard on a horse.'

'One of the guards. They keep horses handy.'

'The dogs are behind, in those buildings?'

'On the extreme left. What can you see?'

'It would take an Olympic runner to make it to the road here,' Macklin said in a vexed voice. 'Mel couldn't do it,' he added grimly. 'I just know he couldn't.'

'Mel thinks he can.'

'How did you figure it when you were down there?'

Ames was consulting his watch. It was five minutes after twelve. 'You'd better lean on the horn.'

'Answer me,' Macklin commanded

sharply. 'What did you think when Mel talked about running to the road?'
'I didn't think it was impossible.'
'By heaven! I believe I can see him . . . '
Ames had heard a sound behind them on the road. He swivelled his head and saw another car, travelling fast. It was sending up clouds of dust.
'Put the glasses away, Art,' he snapped.
'It's him right enough!'
Ames grabbed the binoculars and plucked them from Macklin's eyes. The man swore harshly, then he heard the car too and subsided.
'You're so damned smart, why can't you keep your wits about you?' Ames grated.
The car was a Volkswagen and there was a man at the wheel. He was alone and raced on past them without bothering to glance at thc Oldsmobile. Macklin lifted the binoculars to his eyes again.
'Here, have a gander,' he said after another moment. 'Off to the right. There's a group of five or six prisoners on their own.'
Ames raised the binoculars and tried to

pick them out. The glasses really were powerful, the magnification placing the group of prisoners not more than a dozen yards away. Ames let them freeze on one of the men. His heart skipped a beat and his mouth went dry.

He was looking at Mel Savage.

'It's him all right,' he agreed softly. 'Lean on the horn. But don't make it too obvious.'

'I'll watch and you blow the horn.'

'Do it, chump. I've got eyes as well as you.'

Macklin depressed the horn button and the blast ran over the silence of the countryside. Ames concentrated on Mel Savage. He saw the man jerk and lift his head, his gaze leaping to the distant road above him. Macklin was about to blow again when Ames trapped his hand.

'Lay off. He reacted.'

'You're sure?'

'Of course I'm sure. Sound that once more and there'll be more than Mel reacting. The whole prison will suspect something in the wind. Get out of here fast.'

Macklin reached for the starter and drove rapidly away from the scene. They came to a turnoff where Ames said he could reverse to drive back to Blandon.

'I want to see where the road comes out,' Macklin declared. He continued driving.

'I know where it comes out.'

'You walked up here when you were freed from the prison?'

'No, I didn't. I walked out on to the low road. But this is bound to join with the low road. Ten miles along it to the west and you reach the highway.'

'I'm going to satisfy myself, Lew. Anyhow, it mightn't be wise to retrace our way.'

He did have a point Ames conceded. He lay back on his seat and lit a cigarette. It was roughly five miles to the low road and when they reached it Ames recognised it immediately and pointed.

'That direction takes you to the highway.'

Macklin had halted at the junction and now he appeared to be calculating the time required to make it from the spot where they hoped to pick up Savage to the highway.

'There could be a snag there' he said musingly. 'If the alarm was raised at the prison and the guards moved fast they could block us off here.'

'We could keep on going through the country and join the highway later.' What Macklin said was possible and Ames had no desire to be confronted by a bunch of trigger-happy guards.

'No' Macklin rejoined. 'That could be as risky. I'd meant to give Blandon a wide berth when we left it tomorrow night but we'll head back there with Mel and use the main road from Blandon to reach the highway.'

'What if something slips and Mel doesn't make it?'

Macklin didn't answer him for several seconds. He looked worried — grim might have been the word to describe his expression.

'We'll cross one bridge at a time,' he said finally.

They drove on to the highway and curved back to Blandon. Macklin said little during the remainder of the journey. Ames guessed at what he was thinking. It was all right talking about the prison farm and of Savage making good his escape from it; when you saw the actual prison layout and saw Savage down there digging out rocks you were forced to adopt a different perspective.

They were weaving through the busy streets when the crook broke his silence.

'Mel could have worked on another angle had be been smarter' he said. 'Do you see those trucks?'

'You could have made use of one of them?'

'Right. That's how you and Mel should have planned it. We could have watched the routine gone through by the truck drivers. Then we could have jumped one of the drivers and Dave or I could have taken his place. It would have been a simple matter to smuggle Mel out under a load of rubble.'

'I wouldn't have banked on it,' Ames said: 'Those guards are hawks. Then you or Dave would have been locked up as well.'

‘It’s too late talking about it.’ Macklin looked for a clear stretch of kerb and pulled the Oldsmobile in and switched off the engine.

‘Why are you stopping here?’

‘You’re getting out here, chum. I haven’t forgotten that fat guy. He could gum up the show at the last minute. You can take a cab to your hotel. Here’s what you’re going to do. You and Eve check out of the hotel tomorrow night before eleven. Take your car and follow the route out of town we took earlier. When you reach the outskirts we’ll be there waiting for you. If we’re not waiting, stay where you are until we show up.’

‘You’re not having a formal get-together then? I mean, this would sound better to Eve coming from you.’

‘Don’t give me that crap, Ames. Keep your nose clean until tomorrow night. Now beat it.’

Ames got out of the car and Macklin drove off. At least it had arrived at the stage where they trusted him out of their sight. Or did they? How did he know he wasn’t being watched at this moment, that Huggins, instead of keeping an eye on Eve as they wished him to believe, was actually watching him? And the fat Harold J. Good who was a private investigator. Where did he come into it all? Who was paying his check?

Ames was tempted to call Edward Ogden once more and learn if there were any new developments. He decided not to. He could only lean so heavily on the chief; after that he was supposed to stand on his own feet.

He caught a cab and was driven back to the street where the small hotel was located. He asked the cabbie to let him down two blocks short of the hotel. He walked the rest of the way, and was mildly surprised to notice the dark green Ford still parked on the opposite side of the street.

Dave Huggins roused when he saw him, gave him a thin smile, and started the Ford's engine running. He drove off as Ames entered the hotel lobby.

Ames was in his room for long enough to freshen up when the door was rapped. He opened it and Eve walked into the room. She looked angry about something.

'Did you see Dave parked across the street?' she demanded.

'He isn't there now.'

'No. But he was there all the while you were away. You can see plainly how much they trust me.'

'Why seem so amazed? They don't trust you and they don't trust me. They don't trust themselves, I bet.'

'I wish the hell I was out of this town, Lew. I've got a very bad feeling about this town.'

'It's all in yourself.' Ames summoned a wry grin. 'Aren't you going to ask me about Mel?'

Her breath caught in her throat and she laid a hand on his arm. 'Did — did you actually see him?'

'Sure, I saw him. Art had a set of binoculars along and they made all the difference.'

A little groan escaped Eve and she dropped on to a chair. Ames lit two cigarettes and gave her one. She puffed automatically, her dark eyes never leaving his face.

'Tell me,' she urged.

Ames shrugged.

'What is there to tell? I saw him. Art saw him. Art gave a blast on his horn and it registered with Mel.'

'But will he understand what it is, Lew? Do you think he might have given up hoping? Might he not imagine somebody is playing a trick on him?'

'Not the way I look at it, baby.'

He told her about Macklin's plans for tomorrow night. She listened carefully and nodded slowly when he had finished. Her eyes clung to his like glittering diamonds.

'Do you believe he will make it, Lew?' she whispered.

'He's got an even chance of making it,' was all Ames felt inclined to say.

Eve rose from the chair and came over to offer her lips to him.

'Kiss me, Lew. Then hold me tight. Hold me tight as hell in case I fall to pieces at the last moment.'

16

Ames rose at eight next morning and had his breakfast delivered to his room. Afterwards he left the room and went down in the elevator to the lobby. At the desk he told the clerk he would be checking out that evening. Last night he had arranged this with Eve. He would check out at around ten and she would do the same at ten-thirty. He would wait along the street for Eve to emerge from the hotel and pick her up in his car.

'There hasn't been anyone inquiring for me?' he asked the desk clerk.

'Nobody, Mr Smith.'

He waited to see if the clerk would say anything further, but he didn't. If Harold Good was inquiring about him he would ask for a Mr Ames. Or would he? Good would be smart enough to guess that Ames might assume another name. If the private investigator was hot on his trail, he would stick around and watch him without asking.

Ames wished he could find out a little more about the fat man and the reason for his interest in him. He thought of going to the investigator's office and seeing what he could discover there. But Edward Ogden had warned him against this. Okay. So maybe Ogden was a trifle wiser concerning the affair this morning.

Ames went into the street, halting under the hotel canopy to view the bustling traffic and the people who passed by. He began strolling along keeping his eyes peeled for the fat man or the car he drove. Or Macklin and Huggins or the cars they drove. He stopped again at a corner to get a cigarette going, and when he was satisfied that the coast was clear, continued walking.

He entered the same drugstore he had used to contact Delton City previously. In the booth he called the number and watched the drugstore customers while he waited. It was a minute before he was put through to the chief.

'Ames here, sir. I thought I'd better make a final check with you. Anything fresh on the shamus?'

'Not a thing, Lew,' Ogden said. 'I had our man pay a visit to his office in the role of prospective client. He hires a lady secretary, and all she could say was that Good was working on a case, and had been out of town for weeks.'

Ames whistled softly.

'It would take money to pay a guy for that kind of endeavour, wouldn't it?'

'I see what you mean, Lew. You've got the notion that someone hopes his sprat will catch a mackerel. But Good's secretary said this was nothing strange for her boss. He is offered the oddest assignments, and takes them.'

'That secretary must be holding back. If Good's on an assignment, she ought to be the first one to know about it. She could supply details of whatever arrangements were drawn up between Good and his client. In short, sir, she's bound to have the client's name in her records.'

'But we're using kid-glove methods,' Ogden reasoned. 'You don't want to scare the guts out of everybody, do you? And this is too delicate to handle roughly.

However, I've made other plans to uncover the identity of the client. By morning I might have the information we need.'

Ames knew what he meant. He would have Good's office broken into after dark. But that should have been done last night. In the morning he wouldn't be here. There was no telling where he might be in the morning.

'I haven't seen sign of him since arriving in Blandon,' he said to Ogden. 'Small mercies again, perhaps. What about the fifth member of the outfit?'

'Farland? He's under surveillance at this minute, Lew. He isn't within a hundred miles of where you are. We'll be swooping in shortly.'

'That's something to be thankful for too. By the way, sir, tonight is the night.'

'You don't say. Well, I wish you all the best, Lew. It isn't too late to have our man team up with you.'

'No. Let him carry on with the shamus. He might dig up a surprising item.'

'From what I hear of Blandon, the labourer in the fields doesn't have a dog's chance of getting anywhere. What will you do if he's caught?'

'I'll play it by ear as usual,' Ames said. 'I've got the dame pretty soft on me. If our man fails to make it, there'll be a showdown of some kind or other. All three of them have been sitting on top of a volcano for years. My money says there'll have to be an eruption. At that stage I might ask for Macklin and Huggins to be apprehended. Then I'll have just the woman to contend with.'

'Do your best, Lew. Lots of luck. Goodbye.'

Ames didn't dally long after he'd hung up. Eve Birchall would be living on a high pitch this morning. As soon as she awakened she might want to get in touch with him. If she discovered his absence from the hotel there was no saying what she might think.

He reached the lobby and rode up in the elevator to his room. He remained there for five minutes, then looked out and headed for Eve's room. There was no response to his light tap on the door. He tapped again and tried the handle. The door wasn't locked. Thinking that Eve might have panicked at the last minute, he went in and looked around. Her suitcase was here and so was her extra clothing. Satisfied that Eve had gone out to buy something, he left her room and hurried back to his own.

Ten minutes later there was a summon to the door.

Ames opened it to look at Eve. She was wearing a grey tweed outfit — skirt and jacket, and a light blue cashmere sweater.

She stepped into the room and turned to stare at him.

'Where were you?' she demanded in the taut manner she often adopted. 'I was here earlier and I couldn't get in.'

'That's more than can be said for the way you leave your room,' Ames replied with a faint grin. 'You just turn the handle and walk in.'

'I must have forgotten to lock the door.' She opened her purse and extracted a cigarette. It was a new pack of Camels and Ames guessed she had gone out to buy cigarettes. 'But you haven't answered my question, Lew.'

‘I went for a walk. It’s a nice morning and I had a notion for a breath of fresh air.’

‘I see.’ Her dark eyes shifted from his face. She found a lighter in her purse and lit the Camel. ‘How far did you walk, and what did you do?’

‘I declare I believe you’re getting jealous,’ he kidded and tried to take her into his arms. She evaded him and moved over to stand by the door, her features tight and humourless.

‘Where were you, Lew?’

The timbre of her voice struck an alarm bell for Ames. He saw there was more to the quiz than idle curiosity. He dug around in his head for a story to please here. She had seen him leave his room, of course. She must have followed him to the drugstore to satisfy whatever suspicions concerning him remained with her. How much else did she know?

He spread his hands, allowing the planes of his face to go sober. ‘I might as well tell you,’ he said. ‘I thought a lot about that fat guy through the night. Did you ever have a brilliant inspiration out of nowhere in the middle of the night?'

'We're not discussing my brainstorms,' Eve said coldly. 'Let's hear about yours.'

She was a split personality. Sometimes warm and tender and hungering for sheer animal companionship. Sometimes hard and cold and frighteningly self-sufficient.

'Like I said,' he explained. 'It hit me out of nowhere. This fat guy was somehow tied up with the party I knocked down and killed in my car two years ago. Maybe he was a brother or a cousin of the accident victim. He had figured my two years in prison wasn't ample punishment for what I'd done, and had got on my trail immediately they let me out of the prison farm.'

Eve's expression altered as the possibility started to impress her. A frown gathered up her brows. He had told her a little, but he hadn't told her all. So she must have watched him use the phone in the drugstore.

'Well,' he continued, 'I have a couple of friends in Delton City, strange as it may seem. One of them is Barney Knapp, a journalist. I thought about Barney and I thought about the fat guy. I decided to give Barney a ring and ask him if he could provide any clues regarding the dead man's relations.'

'Could he?'

Ames shook his head. He saw her features relax, the tightness recede from her mouth.

'That could explain it,' she said finally. 'But it still doesn't change the fact that the fat man could mess up what we're working on.'

'He's one man, baby. What can he do?'

She was silent for a moment, then she smiled feebly.

'I suppose you're right, Lew. Oh, hell, I'm an absolute bundle of nerves. I can't wait for night to come round. And then I can't bear to think what might happen when Mel makes his escape bid.'

'You need a drink,' Ames said. 'I can read the signs. Scoot down to the cocktail lounge and I'll join you there in a few minutes.'

'Dare we?'

'Of course we dare. A man and woman

can have a friendly drink together. Anyhow, tonight this dump will be far behind us.'

* * *

At ten he was ready to leave the hotel. He had drawn on his shoulder harness, checked the mechanism of the .38 automatic and placed it in the holster. To offset the probability of someone reading the slight bulge beneath his jacket, he was wearing an old mac without a belt.

He lit a cigarette, rang for the bellhop to come and collect his suitcase, and went down in the elevator to settle his bill.

It was a fine night outside, with a light breeze tugging at the dregs of the day's heat trapped in the street. He stood for several minutes to look around him, then went to collect the Dodge. He drove it to the end of the street and cruised through a few other streets, all the while watching in his driving mirror. He saw nothing to cause him alarm.

Eve came out of the hotel promptly at ten-thirty. Ames had halted a block away and got out to take her suitcase and place it in the trunk. She sat down beside him without saying anything, and he knew by the tense lines of her features that she was strung up to the very limit.

'Take it easy, will you.'

'It's all right for you to talk,' she said snappishly.

'How is it all right for me? We're part of a unit.'

'I'm sorry, Lew. My nerves are giving me gyp. Just drive on and leave me alone.'

Macklin had said eleven, and there was plenty of time to make it to the outskirts of Blandon. He drove slowly, taking the utmost care with the traffic. Eve sat stiff and straight, her eyes fixed steadily ahead of her. At length they were out in the suburbs and the time was drawing on to eleven.

'Where did you plan to meet Art and Dave?'

'Just clear of town,' Ames said.

'How are we going to split up?' she asked him next.

'I can't say. Art and Dave have been working this out without our benefit.'

'I don't trust them, Lew.'

'I know,' he grunted. 'Nor me. Nor yourself likely. But I can't say that I blame you.'

'All the same, I'd like to stick with you,' she went on urgently. 'And they're not going to plant me somewhere to keep me out of the way.'

Ames shrugged and said nothing. She could take it up with Macklin and Huggins. He didn't want to appear too anxious to stick close to her until the plan had gone through. Still, if Savage failed to make it and she heard the dogs baying . . .

He drew into the side of the road and waited. He was accepting one of Eve's cigarettes when he saw the Ford glide past.

'That's Dave! But why didn't he stop?'

'Art is behind.' Ames told her.

She swore softly at the way they were keeping her in the dark. Just when Ames was tempted to tell her to shut up he saw the dim shape of the Olds ease in behind them. Macklin got out and approached the driving side window. His eyes were narrow slits of dull flame.

'Everything okay?'

'If you call Eve having kittens okay, then you're right.'

'What's the matter, baby?'

'Nothing,' she said to Macklin. 'Why is Dave out in front?'

'Because I told him to go out in front,' Macklin replied flatly. 'He's going to drive past the point where Mel should appear. It could happen we might have to block off a section of the road.'

'I'm going to stay with Ames.'

'Stay with him,' Macklin said readily. 'So long as you can restrain yourself. Remember you don't scream. You don't have a tantrum. You play it cool all the way.'

'Isn't it time we were moving?' Ames asked brusquely.

'Sure it is. You know the spot, Lew. If we pick up Mel we turn around and make it hell for leather back to Blandon.'

'Where do we rendezvous?'

'Number eighty-three, Capstick Street. It's just to the east of the hotel where you were staying. We managed to rent a dump for a month.'

'Sharp thinking, Art.'

'You'll learn,' Macklin rejoined cryptically. 'Get going, Lew. I'll be a short distance behind you.'

Macklin left them and Ames drove out from the kerb.

He based his speed on the earlier journey to the road above the prison farm. Mel might manage to make his break at midnight and he might not. All the same, they'd better be at the place by no later than midnight.

The road was relatively free of traffic. Eve chain-smoked until Ames lifted a bottle and handed it to her.

'I was keeping this in reserve. Go on and have a snifter. You're like a cat closed up in a dog pound.'

She reached for the bottle, but then waved it away.

'If I touch that I might empty it, the mood I'm in.'

Forget your mood. See how calm I am. Hold my hand if you feel like it.'

'I wish you'd quit joking, Lew.'

'I'm not joking, honey, believe me. I'm simply whistling in the dark.'

They said nothing for a long time. Then Eve stirred and turned to view the side of Ames' face.

'If something should go wrong . . . ' she said tremulously and stopped.

'Yeah?' he urged without taking his attention from the road racing into his headlamps. 'I'm listening to you.'

'Will — will you stay by me?'

'Against Dave and Art you mean?'

'You know what I mean,' she said passionately. 'Don't you see, Lew, this is the chance they have been waiting for. If we don't manage to rescue Mel and it slips through their fingers — '

'That's when the tide will really turn?' he said gently. 'Yes, I've considered it, Eve. They might turn on you like crazed wolves, demanding that you show them where the loot is hidden, or tell them where it is. They could be two nasty guys if they really blew their cool.'

'Will you do it, Ames?'

'For how much?'

He heard her catch her breath. He glimpsed a headlamp in his driving mirror and guessed it belonged to Macklin's car.

As yet there was no sign of Huggins' car in front of them.

'Mel promised you a hundred thousand dollars.'

'How much would you promise me, Eve?'

'A fifty-fifty cut.'

'No strings?'

'I thought you wouldn't want strings,' she said bitterly.

He reached out and grasped her hand. He gave the slim fingers a hard squeeze.

'It all depends on how you look at it, honey. I could bind myself to you without the help of strings.'

He thought she sobbed drily, but he wasn't sure, nor did he dare to twist his head to look.

'You've got yourself a deal,' he said after a few minutes. 'But don't let those guys suspect anything. If you do we'll both be cooked.'

Ames slowed when he saw headlamps blossoming ahead of him. It was the first vehicle they had met since leaving the fork a couple of miles back. A truck materialised from the shadows and rocked past at breakneck speed.

'Stupid punk,' Ames grumbled.

'Are we nearly there, Lew?'

'We're nearly there.'

Round a corner he saw the faint red glow of a car's rear lights in the distance. He slowed the Dodge to almost a crawl, not wanting to overrun the place where they were supposed to wait. He needn't have worried. Suddenly there was a break in the dark mass of trees below them and he saw a dozen arc lamps away off on the flats. Eve's fingers clutched his arm and gouged in fiercely.

'Is this it, Lew?'

'This is it,' he said and cut the engine. Macklin's car was crawling up behind. His headlamps went dead and Ames killed the Dodge's.

In the gloom he noticed Eve working at the clasp of her purse. Her hand went into it and came out again. Something was glinting in her hand now. The gun she had pulled on him that day when he had first met her.

17

'What are you going to do with that?' he hissed.

'I don't know,' she said dully. 'Having it makes you feel better. I might have to use it. I can handle a gun, you know.'

'You'd better get it out of sight,' Ames warned. 'If Art sees you flashing a rod he's liable to call the whole thing off.'

Eve pushed the gun into her purse again as Macklin approached the Dodge. He asked Ames what time he made it.

'Few minutes off midnight. Four to be exact.'

'I make it the same. If Mel is to try and escape he should be on his way.'

Ames and Eve got out to stand beside Macklin. Macklin swept the terrain below them with binoculars.

'Can you see anything at night with those?' Eve queried. Her voice quavered and Ames could guess at the strain she was being subjected to at this moment.

'They're night glasses,' he said to her.

'It sure is quiet,' Macklin announced after he had looked about him to his satisfaction. 'It seemed a long way down there by daylight. It looks twice as far in the dark.'

Eve made no comment. She was standing on the edge of the road and staring down across the woods to the fields, and beyond where the arc lights cut swathes of silver around the perimeter of the prison compound.

A cool breeze was blowing and brought the scent of fresh-turned earth. The sky had been covered with clouds, but now they began to clear and thousands of stars peeped out. Ames glanced along the road to where Dave Huggins was waiting in the Ford. He would drive the car across the road to block it if Macklin signalled him to do so.

'Can't we do something to help Mel besides standing here?' Eve demanded as the minutes sped by.

'What can we do?' Macklin grunted. 'We don't even know if Mel is going to attempt to escape. You might come here a dozen nights in a row and he wouldn't get the opening.'

'We could go down there and be nearer to him if he does manage to get out,' Eve said stubbornly. 'Couldn't we, Lew?'

'You're nuts,' Macklin said with contempt in his voice. 'Why didn't you stay in town and let us carry this through?'

'I'm going to see,' the woman panted and started forward. Macklin went to grab her to restrain her, but Ames clutched his arm in turn.

'Let her go.'

'Are you crazy too? You talked about the dogs. The guards on their horses. A stupid woman could ruin the whole gag.'

'Sure,' Ames agreed. 'And she might be killed. What would become of the quarter million bucks then?'

'You're right. Okay. Go ahead if you both want to play with fire.'

As Ames was leaving him the crook brought a gun from his pocket. Ames caught up with Eve and spoke roughly to her.

'We're both putting our backs to that guy. And he's talking nothing but the truth. There are dogs down there. There are men on horses. Men with rifles.'

'I've got the feeling that Mel is already out of the prison,' Eve said mechanically. 'He'll need help. If we're close enough we can help him.'

'I'm not allowing you to go far. Mel knows what he has to contend with. Dogs and guards, yes. But a hysterical woman, no. You'll ball it up for him.'

Even as he spoke she tripped and fell. Ames could have saved her from hitting the ground, but he deliberately let her fall. She swore and pushed herself to her feet. Upright, she leaned against him for a moment, peering at the edge of the woods.

'I'm sure I hear something, Lew!'

'You do hear something. My heart beating.'

'Are you scared?'

'I'm scared plenty. If a situation like this didn't scare you, then you're not normal.'

'This will finish me with Art,' she said. 'I could tell by the look he gave me. I think he hates me.'

'You don't go out of your way to endear yourself to him.'

Ames took her hand and they walked across a stubbled field to the edge of the woods. If they wished, they could follow the line of trees until it petered out at the lower fields. Ames didn't think it would be a good idea. He jerked his head to peer back at the road and Macklin. He couldn't see Macklin in the darkness but he could see the outlines of the two cars, and guessed Macklin would have those night-glasses trained on them.

Eve would have gone on when Ames halted. Despite all warnings she had taken the gun from her purse again and was holding it at the ready.

'How did you ever rate a bank-robbing gang?' he grumbled. 'It's a wonder the whole lot of you aren't in prison.'

Her eyes glinted brightly in the shadows.

'Are you going to stand here and exercise your jaws. I — ' She broke off suddenly, pointing dumbly to where the lower fields met with the trees. Ames narrowed his eyes and strained them to pick out what she was indicating.

He fancied he saw a shadow against the faint glow coming from the arc lamps. It was close to the ground and moving fast towards the woods. It reached the woods and vanished. In there somewhere a bird set up a fierce protest.

Eve was moaning softly. She found her voice.

'It's Mel, Lew! He's made it. He's going to make it!'

'Let's get back to the road.'

Ames hadn't thought it was possible. He had a sneaking sympathy for Mel Savage. Everybody sympathises with the underdog, whether they do it secretly or openly. Ames had imagined however that somehow or other the crook's escape bid would have been noticed and quickly thwarted.

Colport could be playing that trick, he realised, holding his hand until the escaper could see freedom within his grasp, then unleashing his guards and the dogs, and making sport of overtaking the prisoner and dragging him back to the compound. It would matter little to

Colport whether the prisoner was dead or half-alive on his return. Another lesson would have been spelled out for the farm inhabitants. It would be a long, long time before the escape attempt would be emulated.

Ames gripped Eve's arm and began to pull her into movement. She refused to budge an inch, telling Ames to join Macklin on the road if he wanted to. He could see her eyes gleaming, the way her bosom was rising and falling. The gun she had remained clutched in her fingers.

There was a crashing noise far down in the undergrowth. Eve snatched herself from Ames' grip. She tore in amongst thc trees.

'Come back, damn you.'

He commenced running after her. His shoe snagged on a bulging tree root and he slammed down into thorny bush. He picked himself up in time to see the woman vanishing amongst the thick shadows.

At that instant a siren began to wail, its terrifying cry rising to a shrill crescendo. At the same time more lights were brought into play, their wide, penetrating beams slashing through the woods like brilliant bars of sunlight.

Dogs barked and the short hairs on Ames' neck stood up on end. Damn the woman. Damn Savage too. He might have known he couldn't make it, might have known that Colport was itching for an opportunity to indulge his sadistic streak.

All three of them could be cornered here by the dogs, torn to pieces before anyone would raise a hand to stop them.

'Eve!' he yelled. 'Where are you?'

He heard the woman scream. She screamed and went on screaming. The dogs were baying madly, closer to the woods now, much, much closer. Also, Ames clearly heard the pounding of horses' hooves. He came up short, the sweat rolling off his brow, trapped in an agony of indecision.

Serve both of them right if they were mauled to death or shot to death. The money might never be found, but at least the gang would be effectively broken, and it would be relatively easy to arrange for the capture of Macklin and Huggins.

What if both men took fright and drove off?

It didn't matter, he realised. His own car was up there on the road. If he started running for the road immediately and kept running, he was sure he could make it.

Eve's demented cry rang through the woods.

'Mel, I'm here. I'm here!'

Swearing, Ames started off in the direction of the cry. The closely-spaced trees impeded him. The brush reached out with thorny spikes to clutch at his clothing, scratching his legs, his arms, his face. He ran and kept running.

The dogs had reached the woods now. They were spilling in through the trees. Another shrill yell from Eve. She was closer than Ames had imagined she was. A shot cracked hollowly. Not the heavy explosion of a rifle, but the weaker, staccato bark of a pistol. More shots drummed amongst the narrow avenues of trees.

His chest heaving, his lungs apparently on fire, Ames burst into a clearing and saw the distracted woman. A man was charging towards her, arms outstretched. Ames saw a massive hound bounding at him. Eve triggered her gun again and the dog threshed down in a writhing heap.

The horsemen had galloped to the edge of the timber and were dismounting. A harsh voice issued instructions.

'Shoot the bastard on sight.'

It was all the telling required for the rifles to open up. Ames saw yet another dog break from a tangle of undergrowth. He didn't think twice about pulling his .38 from its sheath and shooting it. He triggered off two shots to make sure. The dog's back arched in midair and it smashed into the brush.

The marksmen were shooting at random, not certain of the location of the escaper, but pouring a hail of lead over a selected area.

Eve screamed as Mel Savage sagged at her feet. By now Ames had reached them and thrust her back with an oath.

'He's hit,' he said.

'Do something for him! I'll hold them off.'

The big bullet had taken Mel Savage in

the head. He'd died almost simultaneously with the pressure of the guard's trigger. The woman wailed frantically and tried to get to him. Ames held her back.

'He's dead. Get the hell out of here if you don't want to die with him.'

It seemed the moment when the whole thing became real to the woman for the first time. She shuddered, sobbing brokenly. She left the dead man and Ames and began running like a wild creature up through the trees.

Ames went after her.

The siren was lifting and falling, flooding the woods and the surrounding countryside with its heart-chilling alarm. Ames heard men tramping through the trees behind him. A crisp command rang out.

'Halt!'

'It's one of our men.'

'Like hell it is.'

Two rifles exploded, the bullets lancing into the trailing branches that Ames sped past. There was no sign of Eve up ahead of him and he prayed she would maintain her sense of direction. Should she falter or turn about she would speedily fall victim to the bellowing rifles.

The dogs seemed to be everywhere, loose and slavering for the prey their nostrils scented. Their frenzied barking and baying was the most hideous noise Ames had ever heard in his life.

He saw a racing shadow in front of him. Eve. She lost her balance and went down. Ames reached her and hauled her to her feet. She was hanging on to the gun like grim death.

'Don't stop,' he panted.

'My ankle. I've twisted it.'

He broke into a run and dragged her along with him. Suddenly they were at the edge of the timber; now they were free of it, and only the stubbled field separated them from the road.

How they reached his car Ames was never to remember clearly. It did register that his was the only car in sight. But he didn't care. So long as the road was clear for him to drive.

He hauled the door open and flung Eve on to the passenger seat. Then ran round and slammed in behind the wheel. The engine fired at once, partially wiping out the keen and wail of the siren. Two guards surged from the trees, dogs tearing past them. Bursts of orange flame stabbed the shadows. A bullet struck the hood and ricochetted off it. Ames reversed recklessly, mounting the road shoulder, facing the car towards Blandon. He tramped his foot on the gas pedal, screeching into a higher gear.

After a few miles his thoughts calmed. Perhaps Macklin and Huggins had taken off to elsewhere. He didn't think they would, though. They would cling to the hope that Eve might save herself, that she still might provide the key to the quarter million.

At this stage another thought intruded. Should he make any manner of effort to link up with the pair? Now that Eve knew there was no future for her with Mel Savage, ought he not utilise this fact to urge her to take off with him and share the money?

'Where are you going, Lew?'

She was dry-eyed and her voice was surprisingly calm and controlled. He lit a cigarette and tossed her the pack.

'At the moment we're heading for Blandon. Do you want to change our destination and go some place else?'

'No,' she said flatly. 'Go to the address in Blandon Art mentioned.' She fumbled out a cigarette and managed to light it.

'They developed ants in their pants, honey. They lit a shuck. Heaven knows to where.'

'We'll try the house all the same. That riot would have scared anybody. I've hit the bottom of the barrel, Lew. I'm dried up.'

'Meaning?' he probed gently.

'I'm going to tell them where the money is. We're going to split it. Equally four ways.'

'What has become of your ambition?'

'There isn't any. I'm dried up, I tell you. Money isn't everything. When you get right down to it, money isn't anything.'

It was a mood that might pass, Ames thought. Yet he wasn't so sure. Mel's death had affected Eve as nothing else could have done. It meant that his own plans were in the greatest jeopardy. He found himself hoping that Macklin and Huggins would have had the skids put under them to the extent of them travelling far beyond Blandon. He would soon see. If he didn't hit a roadblock before he reached the town.

Oddly enough, there was no sign of anything on the road to impede them; neither did he see traffic behind them. He realised he had been pushing the Dodge at seventy and braked sharply at the restricted speed area marking the outskirts of Blandon.

'I can't believe we've made it,' Eve murmured.

'Well, we have. I feel I've been in a king-size nightmare. How about your ankle?'

'It's all right. I just twisted it.'

It took Ames twenty minutes to find Capstick Street. It was little more than an alley, with the minimum of lighting at that hour of the night. Ames cruised the Dodge until he was opposite eighty-three. His mouth went dry when he saw the Ford and the Oldsmobile choking up the narrow driveway.

It was a small, single-storied house, and the front door opened as soon as they reached it. Art Macklin stared blankly at them.

'I figured you were both dead.'

'A hell of a lot you cared,' Ames growled.

'Leave him alone, Lew,' Eve admonished.

In the hall Huggins appeared with a gun in his hand. Macklin asked them about Mel.

Eve couldn't speak and it was Ames who told him.

'All blazes broke loose,' Macklin lamented. 'You can't blame us for taking off, Eve.'

'Nobody's blaming you,' she said hollowly.

In the tiny living room Huggins produced whisky and glasses. Ames swallowed a large slug at a gulp, as did Eve.

'We can't stay here,' Macklin said. 'We can't stay together either.' He was primed for business and Ames could guess what was on his mind. It was significant that Huggins hadn't put his gun away, but laid it on the table at his side.

'I know all that.' Eve sighed. 'Don't

worry, Art. I've quit playing hard to get. We're going to collect the money. We're going to share and share alike. That's the only condition I'm going to lay down and stick to.

Macklin and Huggins exchanged glances. Huggins lifted his shoulders and looked at Ames.

'What does the big guy say to that?'

'It wasn't how the cards were dealt,' Ames objected.

'It was a bum deal,' Macklin rasped. 'It was no deal at all. You take what you get, sonny boy, and you be hellish grateful that you get that much.'

'I mean it, Lew,' Eve said firmly.

He hesitated a moment and then nodded.

'I know when to cut my losses.'

'Where's the money at, Eve?' Macklin asked her.

She finished her drink and searched for another cigarette.

'It didn't leave Maytown,' she declared. 'I never told you, but I have a married sister there. She's married to a respectable store manager. They own a big house, a house with an attic. I left the suitcases there with the promise from Laura that they wouldn't be touched until I returned for them.'

Sweat glistened on Macklin's brow and upper lip. He snapped a lighter for Eve.

'Your sister's name?'

'She doesn't have to tell you,' Ames cut in. 'She'll take you there. A straight deal it is and a straight deal it's going to be.'

Eve waved a hand at him.

'It's all right, Lew. Laura wouldn't part with the cases to anyone but me. Her name is Davenport. She lives at — '

Eve stopped speaking at a gesture from Huggins. The swarthy man had heard something outside the shuttered window. He grabbed his gun. Macklin produced his.

'Somebody sneaking round back,' Huggins whispered. 'Keep talking and I'll slip out front and see.'

'It might be the police!' Eve choked.

'Take it easy,' Macklin hissed. 'Go on, Dave. I'll see you to the door. Ames, you keep gabbing if Eve can't.'

It was impossible for Ames to form a

word with his tongue. It appeared to be glued to the roof of his mouth. Eve's eyes were dark caverns of fear. Her face was a white mask.

The two men seemed to be gone for an age when scuffling in the hall sent him to the door of the room. Huggins was prodding a man inside with the muzzle of his gun. Ames' blood chilled to ice as he recognised the fat man who had been following him.

'Go on,' Huggins grated. 'Get in there and tell us what it's all about.'

'You can't do this to me,' Good bleated. 'I wasn't doing any harm. A friend of mine used to live here and I thought he was still living here.'

'And you had the habit of sneaking in at the back door?' Huggins sneered.

'No, no! You don't understand . . . '

'Damn right I don't, pal. But you're going to make me understand.'

He gave Good a heave that sent him lurching over a sofa.

Eve had backed into a corner and couldn't tear her gaze from the private detective. Macklin came into the room and stood with his shoulders to the door.

'It's him, Lew,' Eve said hoarsely. 'It's the same man.'

'The guy who was tailing you?' Macklin demanded. 'Well, isn't this a turn-up for the book!'

Ames didn't say anything. He watched Harold Good gather himself off the sofa and turn to stare at him. The fat man was quivering like a jelly.

'Don't let them harm me,' he said to Ames. 'I was only doing my job. I work strictly inside the law.'

Macklin's brows knitted in puzzlement as he regarded Ames.

'I thought you didn't know him, Lew.'

'I don't know him.'

'I've got a funny feeling he knows you.'

Ames ran his tongue over his lips. His lips were like lumps of cardboard. He tried to bring all his schooling to bear. Eve too was looking at him curiously now.

A mirthless laugh escaped the swarthy Huggins.

'Do you know something, folks. I've got the strangest smell in my nose. Kind of rat smell.'

He moved slowly to Good and the fat man retreated until he was up against the wall. There was a framed picture hanging there that his shoulder knocked to the floor. It caused him to jump.

Huggins brandished his gun in the detective's face.

'Hoist them,' he ordered. 'Go on, fat boy, or I'll spill your guts on the furniture.'

Good lifted his hands above his head. Huggins frisked him. He drew a Colt automatic from the bulging waistband and flipped it to the waiting Macklin. Next he brought a wallet from his jacket and passed this to Macklin as well.

'Give us a run-down, Art.'

Macklin thumbed through the wallet. The first thing he brought to light was a photostat of Good's licence. He whistled softly.

'What d'you know! Private eye.'

'Light begins to dawn. What else is there?'

'Nothing to shout about. A few bucks. A snapshot of a dame.'

'Let's get this over with,' Eve contributed briskly. 'Every minute we wait here it gets the more dangerous.'

'You're right, baby.'

Huggins jabbed his gun into the fat stomach. Good's mouth went slack and rubbery.

'Why were you following Lew around, shamus?'

'I — I — I can't tell you. Its confidential.'

'You must be kidding.'

Huggins smashed the knuckles of his left hand against Good's nose. Blood poured. Tears sprang to the man's eyes.

'Why were you following Lew Ames around?'

'I was hired to do it.'

'That figures, shamus. But who hired you?'

'There'll be trouble if I tell you.'

'Not half as much as there'll be if you don't tell me,' Huggins threatened. He struck the man again, this time in the midriff. Good retched.

'Take it easy,' Ames said tautly.

'Lay off, Lew. This concerns you. This you ought to be glad to hear. Are you going to talk, friend?'